A BROWNSTONE SOLUTION

A BROWNSTONE SOLUTION

ALISON BROWNSTONE™ BOOK TEN

JUDITH BERENS   MARTHA CARR   MICHAEL ANDERLE

L M B P N

DISRUPTIVE IMAGINATION

LMBPN Publishing
PMB 196, 2540 South Maryland Pkwy
Las Vegas, NV 89109

First US edition, June 2019
Version 1.02, November 2020
Print ISBN: 978-1-64202-349-7

A BROWNSTONE SOLUTION TEAM

Thanks to the JIT Readers

Daniel Weigert
Diane L. Smith
Shari Regan
Jeff Goode
Peter Manis
Dave Hicks
Jeff Eaton
John Ashmore
Paul Westman
Dorothy Lloyd
Nicole Emens

If we've missed anyone, please let us know!

Editor
SkyHunter Editing Team

DEDICATIONS

From Martha

To everyone who still believes in magic
and all the possibilities that holds.
To all the readers who make this
entire ride so much fun.
And to my son, Louie and so many wonderful friends who
remind me all the time of what
really matters and how wonderful
life can be in any given moment.

From Michael

To Family, Friends and
Those Who Love
To Read.
May We All Enjoy Grace
To Live The Life We Are
Called.

CHAPTER ONE

Alison leaned over the railing of the ship and stared out at the frothy wind-churned waters of Puget Sound. The frigid wind slapped at her cheeks and dark clouds threatened rain. A light frosting of snow had coated Seattle when they departed, but the city and any hint of snow were long out of sight. January on the ocean did not make for pleasant travel.

Light pulsed beneath the surface on the sides and behind the long gray NOAA research vessel that plowed through the water. A shimmering triangular sheet of light streaked ahead in front of the ship, and a strand of blue-yellow light connected it to the bow. It was bait for the magical sea creatures now surrounding the vessel, the sources of the lights in the water.

A smiling brown-haired woman slipped a wand into a holster at her belt before she zipped her ankle-length black raincoat and stepped to the railing. "Do you see any trouble?"

Alison shook her head. She pointed to a few black

specks high above them. "I have my team watching us with drones. We should be fine, Dr. Masterson. I have my best people aboard. Even if anything happens, we'll be able to handle it."

"Dr. Masterson?" The woman waved her hands in front of her chest. "I told you before, call me Kailee. I hate it when people call me Doctor Masterson, even when I go to conferences." She gestured to one of the light pulses. "I didn't really make it clear before, but now that we're underway, I want to say I was ecstatic when I heard we would have Brownstone Security to help protect the Shimmer Rays while we lead them to the sanctuary." She laughed. "I joked about getting your company when I proposed the transfer of the Shimmer Ray population, but I didn't think we'd be able to afford it. I have to thank you for the discount. I understand it's something you don't do often."

"It's nice to do a job that doesn't involve crazy terrorists every now and again, and when my assistant mentioned it, it seemed like a good idea. Then again, from what you've told me, many of these poachers work directly for organized crime groups. So it's merely another day at the office for me." Alison looked over her shoulder to make sure none of her friends were on the deck, clutching their stomachs and losing their lunch.

Mason, Drysi, and Hana stood inside the squat bridge. The fox had a little trouble with balance for the first few hours of the trip, but a quick spell by Mason took care of that. She currently stood near the Welsh woman, laughing at something.

Kailee sighed. "It's sad that we even need protection,

but poaching activity is what has forced us to move the population. I might be a witch, but it's not exactly like NOAA wants their scientists to confront magical poachers. Besides, I lack the practical fighting experience your team has."

From what the woman had explained, Shimmer Rays were hunted because their organs were useful ingredients in a number of magical preparations, both ritual components and potions.

"Don't worry about the poachers." Alison shrugged. "I have a reputation. It might be enough to keep us from running into any sort of trouble at all. And you have everything secured on the Canadian end?"

The scientist nodded. "According to the last transmission we received, the Canadian security team will meet with us shortly after we pass into Canadian territorial waters. They'll take us the rest of the way, but only because their government prefers it that way. I wouldn't have minded you going all the way with us, and I do appreciate you being here for even this short period. I feel far safer knowing the famous Alison Brownstone is on board."

Kailee smiled as one of the Shimmer Rays leapt out of the water. The animal resembled a translucent Manta Ray cloaked in a secondary skin of shimmering white light, although the animal lacked the eyes and mouth of a mundane ray. It reentered the water and dove several yards.

"I don't think a lot of people realize how precarious the situation is for so many of these magical animal populations," she explained. "It'll probably be hundreds if not thousands of years before the background level of magic on Earth is sufficient to support healthy populations of such creatures. It's almost a miracle that there is a breeding population of these beautiful animals as is, and I've spent my entire career trying to protect them. Actually, they were the subject of my doctoral thesis. They are a distinct species compared to the Shimmer Rays on Oriceran, but funding's a lot less tight these days, which helps."

"It is?" Alison regretted how skeptical she sounded. "I don't really follow academia. Sorry."

The woman nodded. "Ever since they identified that Mallaoch a few years back, there's been far more awareness of the issue of protecting magical creatures. Awareness brings money."

Alison had heard about it. A Mallaoch was a massive marine creature that could easily be mistaken for an island, and a group composed primarily of students—some of whom were from the School of Necessary Magic, which gave her a warm feeling of pride—had found one off the east coast during an otherwise routine magical survey trip. Even many Oricerans were excited by the discovery of such a rare beast, let alone one on Earth.

She had been to Oriceran but most people on Earth hadn't. Kailee was right. The more magic that flowed into Earth, the more the planet would change into a world of magic and what used to be considered fantasy, and people underestimated what that would mean. Even though most people understood that Oriceran was a world of high magic, they often thought of magic as nothing more than a fancy new toy they could use and not as a fundamentally reality-changing force.

What will the world look like in a hundred years? Two

hundred years? I kick a lot of ass, but people like Kailee change the world in their own very important way by protecting our new magical heritage.

"A witch scientist, huh?" Alison smiled. "I was thinking about how people get so stuck in their head about what magic means, but I'm no better. I'm a security contractor who deals mostly with magical threats. Even though I went to a school from where most magicals went on to less violent work, I let myself forget that not every magical's out there fighting."

Kailee rested her arms on the railing. "My family was fully aware of their magical heritage even before the gates opened, and we usually managed to produce one solid witch or wizard, if not more, each generation. I was born the year the gates started opening, actually." She released a wistful sigh. "I grew up wanting to live on Oriceran so badly, a true world of magic. We took a few trips there when I was younger, but it was weird. It's…magical, but it's also very alien in its own way. Still, seeing so many magical creatures inspired me to help protect what we have on Earth."

She smiled. "I knew it'd be hard. Most of the funding for this kind of thing is governmental, and even the private funding tends to be geared toward people who already rely heavily on government projects. There was still considerable concern about magicals when I started graduate school." She chuckled. "Even today, it's not as if NOAA is full of magicals, and being a marine biologist isn't the best-paying job in the world, especially for a witch."

Alison glanced at Tahir and Sonya's four drones circling overhead. "I suppose we all end up where we need to be in the end." She frowned as a wave of magic passed through her. There was a high level of local magic from the bait, but the latest sensation was distinct from that.

Kailee swallowed and pulled out her wand. "Did you feel that?"

"Yeah, I did." She sighed and tapped her ear to make sure her receiver was still in place. "Tahir, do you pick anything up? I felt some strange magic."

"Even accounting for the Shimmer Rays, there was an unusual heat signature in the water," the infomancer replied. "But it simply disappeared."

"Great." She sighed. "So much for my reputation scaring poachers off."

Mason, Drysi, and Hana emerged from the bridge, all grim-faced, but the seriousness was somewhat undercut by Hana's ridiculous bright red vinyl raincoat and matching floppy hat and rubber boots, her version of appropriate sailing wear. The *tachi* rested in its sheath on her sword belt.

Another powerful surge of magic passed over the area.

"Something's coming toward the boat, and fast," Tahir reported.

The entire craft shuddered and almost knocked Alison off her feet. The rays began to scatter.

Kailee gasped and chanted a quick spell. Her bait spell grew brighter, and the rays turned toward it. "I can't let them scatter. They'll be picked off easily, even by other animals, if they leave the group."

With a groan, the vessel listed to one side and something dark leaked from below-deck and spilled into the water. The vessel's captain shouted in the bridge to one of his men. Several rushed toward stairs at the back.

Alison grimaced. "Drysi, how good are you at repair spells?"

"I'm decent." The witch shrugged. "I'm no mechanic, but it's how I saved on my bike whenever some bloody bastard trashed it."

The half-Drow layered a shield over herself and pointed to the stairs. "Go help them plug whatever hole is down there."

"Right." The witch gave a quick nod and rushed away without a backward glance.

Kailee's jaw tightened as she cast another spell. A juddering line of bright white light streamed from her wand to the bait. "It keeps weakening. I think they're trying to remove it. It's definitely poachers."

"Damn." Alison summoned a shadow blade.

Mason drew his wand and cast his shield and enhancement spells. Hana tapped her crystalline ring three times to summon the crimson glow that would protect her. A moment later, her eyes turned vulpine, and her nine glowing tails appeared. She didn't draw her sword but instead, extended her claws.

Four blue flashes erupted from the water. They obliterated the drones in bright explosions.

"We've lost—" Tahir began.

"Yeah, I saw that," Alison interrupted. "Contact the Coast Guard. Let them know we're under attack and attempting to contain the situation. If the assholes destroy the boat, we'll need someone to rescue everyone."

Kailee narrowed her eyes. She grasped her wand with both hands as she strained to maintain her spell.

Streams of water hurtled from the ocean and landed on the deck where they formed into opaque humanoid shapes.

"What the hell are those?" Hana asked as she crouched with her claws up. "These are the poachers? Weird...water guys? Water men? Waterlings?"

Alison shook her head. "No, these are simply summoned garbage—basically dolls. I made a...waterling like this once in school in a class, or whatever you want to call it." She released her sword and thrust out with her palm. A surge of light magic struck one of the figures in the chest. It collapsed into a puddle of regular water and spread over the deck around it. "They aren't so tough. I'm beginning to think our poachers don't know Brownstone Security is on board. That might explain why they've made an attempt."

More jets of water shot from the ocean to form additional invaders.

Huh. The boat isn't listing anymore. Drysi must have succeeded, but the poachers might shoot it again. I have to stop that.

Hana charged forward and swiped her claws through one of the summoned entities. After two passes, it collapsed. A waterling swung its stub of an arm at her to strike her on the side of the head. She stumbled back with a hiss, but the red glow around her remained undimmed.

"They're stronger than they look," she muttered.

Mason chanted something under his breath before he aimed his wand at an enemy and launched a fireball. The attack reduced the target to a puddle.

"Why do I have a feeling we'll be bailing water by the time this is done?" Alison asked. She eliminated another few with quick magical blasts, but additional streams of water launched from the ocean to produce more enemies.

Hana ripped into another two before she shook her head. "This is endless. Why don't they give up already?"

Kailee took several deep breaths and sweat mingled with the water splashed on her face. "I'm keeping all the rays here, but I don't know how long I can maintain this."

"That's probably their plan," Alison suggested. "They're here for the rays, after all, not to take this boat." She took a deep breath as a crazy plan snuck into her mind. "Mason, Hana, can you handle these things for a while?"

The fox rushed through several of the watery attackers and destroyed a couple of them with a few quick swipes. "Sure. We've got this."

"Yes, we're fine, A, but what about you?" Mason's blast reduced another waterling to a puddle. "You've got a plan?"

Alison nodded toward the water as she destroyed two of the entities with shots from both hands. "Why fight the puppets when you can fight the puppet master?"

"True, but…wait, you're planning to go into the water?" He frowned. "Without us?"

"I don't have to wave a wand around, and Hana's speed won't be useful underwater." She grinned. "And whoever is screwing with us is under there." She layered an additional shield around her before she dived over the side.

Tahir really needs to get submarine drones.

CHAPTER TWO

Kailee dropped to one knee, her jaw tight as she continued to feed magic to her bait spell. Sweat mingled with the water already on her face.

We need to keep these things away from her, Hana thought. *And we need to buy Alison time.*

The half-Drow splashed into the ocean as the fox slashed through a waterling. She rushed forward to shred more of the advancing enemies, a satisfied smirk on her face. Destroying mindless summoned water dolls was more fun than shredding mobsters. It was almost like a game. It merely happened to be one that would end with them all dead if they lost.

The water on the deck started to coalesce into new entities.

"Oh, come on. That's not fair." She exhaled a hiss of irritation. At least the mobsters had the decency to either stay dead or down, not form into new mobsters. An image of several shredded suits forming into new tiny Eastern

Union members cut through her irritation, and she laughed. "Tiny Eastern Union members!"

"What are you talking about?" Tahir asked over the comms. "The Eastern Union is there? I've interfaced with some of the ship cameras, and I only see what appear to be some sort of water humanoid."

"No, no. It's nothing. It's only a funny thing I thought about. I don't know why I imagine them as tiny. Don't worry, babe. If you can see us, you know we totally have this situation under control, even if it is annoying."

A waterling swung at her, and the fox ducked the blow before she reduced her latest adversary to a puddle with her counterattack. She needed to focus. The horde might be weak, but if they maintain a constant attack, the teammates would quickly become overwhelmed or enemies would make it past them to attack Kailee or the crew. The waterlings might not exactly be special forces in power armor, but they hit hard, and unshielded non-magical people wouldn't last long against them.

Between trying to sink it and the stupid water monsters, these poaching jerks planned to murder everyone on the ship. Not cool.

Hana sprinted forward and carved through several figures in one attack. Before, it seemed like there were two new waterlings for every one she killed, but now, the number seemed closer to three. She needed to increase the efficiency of her attacks somehow.

Mason stood farther back, aimed, and fired small fireballs. Each attack killed an enemy—although killed seemed too strong a word—but the combined Brownstones' efforts hadn't thinned their ranks at all.

Alison had better hurry, or this entire boat will sink simply from all the water on it.

A glowing red dagger whistled past her and exploded in a cluster of four adversaries. Half of them dissipated as steam while the last trace of their watery remains coated the deck for a moment, then pooled together for a new round of battle.

The fox glanced over her shoulder. Drysi jogged up the deck and frowned as she drew another dagger.

"Did you get the ship fixed?" Hana asked.

The witch nodded. "I won't lie. It's not a tidy, quick repair, but it'll hold enough for the crew to do their thing. I heard over my receiver that Alison was going into the water, so I thought I'd come up and help out against these water bastards."

Mason eliminated a waterling with a point-blank fireball delivered to its featureless head. "Don't waste your daggers. These guys keep coming and coming. We only need to stall them until Alison finds the source."

"They're boarding on the back of the ship now, too," Tahir reported.

The life wizard spun and launched another fiery missile aft to reduce an invading entity to a splash.

"Damn it," Drysi muttered. "Next time, maybe we don't fight the entire bloody ocean."

Hana ripped the *tachi* from its sheath and cut through three waterlings in a single swing. "Okay, it's time to get serious. I've got this up here. I'll protect Kailee."

"Then we'll keep the bastards off the other parts of the ship." Mason nodded and jogged along the starboard side of the vessel.

The witch shook her head and muttered something in Welsh before she raced around the bridge on the opposite side. The two magicals continued their frustrating assault against their summoned foes.

The fox grinned and twirled her blade. The monsters might constantly regenerate, but they were easy to cut down. "I can do this all day," she shouted into the ocean. "Or at least until my anti-seasickness spell wears off." She thrust forward to impale another adversary. It collapsed into a puddle in front of her. "So hurry up, boss lady."

Alison channeled magic into her legs to jet through the water with a steady thrust, her new magical shield reducing some of the drag, It also helped to keep air in without an active filtering spell. She didn't achieve the speeds she could in the air, but she definitely moved faster than she could swim.

I bet if I practiced and thought about it, I could really find a way to move fast, but I don't need to worry about that now. I only need deal with whoever we're up against.

The glow of the rays above barely penetrated the darker, deeper water as she circled under the slow-moving research vessel. When she'd entered the water, she'd glimpsed the likely source of the attack. No clever tracking or lights spells were needed as she closed on something glowing in the distance.

Streams of light fired from a large ring of shining cerulean metal, easily a yard in diameter and not exactly a budget toy artifact. The jets contorted and wiggled as if they were swimming from the artifact toward the surface. Another steady source of magic made her skin tingle. She wasn't sure if it was from the ring or something else. With the streams, the artifact, and residual magic from her team above, she couldn't pinpoint it easily.

I'm underwater protecting glowing rays from poachers while weird water men attack the ship. Huh. Some days are plain weird, even by my standards.

Something else glittered ahead near the ring, and Alison slowed, her eyes narrowed. She thrust her arm forward and launched a white energy lance. It cut through cleanly to vaporize the liquid around it before the ocean itself filled the void, but the attack didn't seem to slow at all. The lance passed above the ring, struck the shining area, and exploded, the sound muffled by the deep water.

Dots of green grew and spread as if painting an object into existence in front of her. It took only a couple of seconds to reveal a glowing green glass sphere that contained three dark humanoid figures she couldn't make out in detail at a distance. The large orb rested atop a triangular silver platform.

Huh. A magical submarine? I guess that makes sense. I'm not underwater enough to keep track of this kind of thing. I'm sure the Navy already has a system to deal with these.

Alison took a breath, grateful for the oxygen as she floated beneath the frigid January waters of the sound, protected from the chill by her layers of shields and the heat trapped inside.

The submarine backed away a few yards and a few bubbles rose behind it. White orbs appeared on two sides of the triangular base. They cast two piercing beams of light that illuminated her.

Damn it. It's not like I can really talk to them underwater, but they have to realize now that this isn't about them attacking a NOAA boat with a marine biologist witch onboard. They have to realize they're outclassed.

She glanced up. The NOAA ship continued to move at a steady if meandering pace, and the Shimmer Rays still swarmed and focused on Kailee's bait. Alison wanted the men to surrender, but at the same time, she also wasn't prepared to let them escape. They'd attempted to sink the research ship and their waterlings could easily have killed everyone on board.

First things first. I need to stop their stupid monster machine. They must have a charging time or something for whatever big spell they used earlier. Otherwise, they would have followed-up already.

Three quick light flares erupted from her hands. The metal ring didn't explode or melt under her attacks, but its light dimmed and the blue streams destined to become waterlings ceased. A few seconds later, the ring's light died completely, and the artifact began to sink.

Okay, assholes. You have no monster factory, and you have an entire team of magicals defending that ship. Surrender already. Today's not your day. Sometimes, you draw the short straw and go to prison.

Arcs of blue-white energy danced across the base of the submarine as the magical pressure built.

This can't be good.

Alison gritted her teeth and shunted additional energy into her side to provide a quick burst of lateral movement.

The dodge saved her from a direct strike from the beam that emerged from the submarine. She spun, zig-zagged with hasty movements, and launched a series of light magic blasts at the poacher's vessel.

Her attacks exploded against the outside of the sphere. The glass didn't crack or separate from the base, but the vehicle's glow faded and the white headlight orbs vanished. It began to sink. The side slid open and three figures swam out. Almost instantly, new light orbs appeared around them.

With the active light above them, she could discern their features better. Two appeared to be humans—wizards, she assumed, as they clutched wands—but then she noticed gills.

Huh. I didn't think of that, but then again, transfiguration's never been my thing. There's something about having magic you can simply shove more power into. Maybe I'm still stuck with dry-land thoughts. But that means they're exposed to the water and don't have the freedom of movement I do with my air layer.

The wizards kicked toward the surface as the third figure grew closer to Alison at a decent speed. He was a yellow-eyed, slit-pupiled humanoid with a thick, scaly hide and a large tail. Sharp claws tipped the creature's fingers. Red-blue striations over his otherwise gray scales helped her identify his species.

Huh. A Nerak? It's my day for rare Oriceran marine creatures, apparently, but this lizard-guy can think, unlike the Shimmer Rays, so he should know better. Damn it.

She barreled toward the wizards and ignored the Nerak for now. She wasn't sure if her standard stun bolt spell would travel well underwater, but it was hard to miss if you actually touched someone. The creature turned and continued to swim toward her. Even without magical propulsion, he achieved good speed.

Alison continued her approach on her targets and shoved magical energy into her fist as she advanced. They tried to move their wands for a spell, but the water kept the movements imprecise and languid. Magic wasn't always a forgiving force, and today, that was true. Whatever spell they intended failed entirely.

One man's eyes widened as she drove her fist into his face and blue-white energy surged through his body. His head jerked and his eyes rolled up toward the back of his head. His partner twisted his wand and arm, but the water again slowed his movements. He had barely managed to aim before she pounded a stun fist into his stomach.

The magic might resemble electricity, but it didn't seem to behave in exactly the same way. She'd never thought much about the exact physics of it.

For marine poachers, you aren't so tough. You're too used to not having to deal with anyone real or simply killing some poor Shimmer Rays.

Alison turned. The Nerak had closed the distance during her wizard encounter. The lizardman ripped at her with his claws. His movements were rapid and fluid and the water didn't slow him as much as his less scaly partners. Her shields held under the first few attacks, but he managed to cut through and reach her shoulder with his next assault. The cold water rushed over her body and immediately numbed her wound, and she kicked back and ensured there was an air bubble around her head as she glared at the Oriceran.

Her adversary tilted his head and slid his claws over each other. A threat, perhaps.

Okay, anti-magic claws. Nobody ever mentioned that about Nerak. Now, I know.

The lizardman charged again, his claws raised. She didn't exactly know how to read his face, but she was convinced there was something smug about the wide-mouthed expression. Either that, or he intended to try to take a bite out of her with his razor-sharp teeth.

Nice try, asshole, but this time, I know what to expect.

Alison channeled magic behind her to burst toward him as she drew energy into her hand. She met his head with her fist. His body jerked as the energy arced visibly over him. He floated, his limbs loose, and she released a deep breath. This fight had been close enough to the surface that the water wasn't pitch black. The idea of having to go deeper made her stomach tighten.

All this magic and tech, and there's still so much stuff out there that might be a surprise. I think I prefer to stay on land.

She grasped the three stunned poachers and swam upward, straining as she cleared the water and the weight of three human-sized creatures dragged her down. With the aid of her now activated shadow wings, she managed to rise out of the water but grunted with each yard gained.

It took a fair amount of additional magic to her wings, but she made it to the bow area. She dumped the three poachers without ceremony. Their unconscious bodies thudded against the hard, water-logged deck.

Alison looked around. Hana stood with both hands around the hilt of her *tachi*, her breathing ragged. Mason and Drysi rushed toward her, their wands at the ready.

Kailee knelt on the deck, her wand in her hand but resting beside her. She was pale and dragged deep breaths in.

"I destroyed the artifact generating those water guys," the half-Drow explained. "At least I thought I did." She looked around. There was no sign of any waterlings. She gestured to the drooling and unconscious poachers. "And I found these guys, too. Did everything go okay up here?"

The fox sheathed her blade and tapped her ring three times. The crimson glow suffusing her skin vanished. A moment later, she took a deep breath and her claws retracted, her tails vanished, and her eyes returned to normal. "That was annoying." She gestured around the deck. "And there's water everywhere. I get it, it's a boat." She shrugged. "But too much water even for a boat."

"We can clean some of that up in a minute." Alison nodded toward the downed men. "I think they expected a few guys with guns, not a mixed team of magical security contractors."

Hana smirked. "Thugs don't have any sense of imagination these days."

Kailee stood and her knees buckled slightly before she recovered. Her wand slipped but she managed to snag it before it fell. She shook her head and sighed. "A Nerak? It's unfortunate that an ocean-dwelling Oriceran race would help with this. I would have hoped that they, of all creatures, would have been an ally in proper ocean management." Her face tightened with anger.

Alison shrugged. "There's scum all over, but it looks like we've stopped the main threat. We should wait and hand them over to the Coast Guard. I think it'll annoy the Canadians less." She pointed over at the pulses marking the

Shimmer Rays. "But you kept most of them together. Maybe even all of them."

Kailee smiled and weariness lined her forehead. She holstered her wand and walked over to the railing. "We kept them safe together. Thank you, Alison. I couldn't have done this without your team."

"No problem." She scratched her cheek and looked at Mason. "We might need to develop some sort of water training program. There are many practical considerations to fighting underwater that don't come up in our normal practice."

He snickered. "I don't think this kind of job will come up all that often."

Hana sighed. "I hope not." She patted her sides. "Although I do love my outfit."

CHAPTER THREE

A few days later, Alison took a deep breath as she stared at the modest two-story brown house perched on the top of the hill. Her heart thundered in her chest, and she glanced back at her Fiat as she wondered if it made more sense to get in and drive away. She wasn't sure if she was ready to confront the two magicals inside.

This is a mistake, but there's no way I can back out. What excuse would I use? I can't say I'm afraid. Not of these two, of all people.

Mason chuckled nervously beside her. "I'm glad you agreed to this. I wasn't sure if you would. I thought you would make up an excuse and was half-prepared to fake believing it, too."

Damn. He sees right through me.

"This is dangerous." She shook her head. "I should have brought backup. Fair enough, you're here, but it's not like you can stand up to them given your relationship."

"I can stand up to them. This honestly won't be as bad as you expect." His chuckle became a more natural laugh.

"And backup? Like who? Hana or Drysi? Ava? I don't think this is the kind of situation where having more firepower —or girl power—really helps. It's not like the two people in that house are anyone you can win against with over-whelming strength. You'll simply need to be diplomatic. You can do this. I know you can."

"At least I'm dressed for the part. I think." Alison sighed and looked down at the open front of her long black coat. Beneath it, she wore a light-blue dress—attractive, on the elegant side, and not too sexy. Mason's briefing on the situation was woefully inadequate. She wanted to be angry with him, but she understood that he was as nervous as she was.

He wore a dark blue suit that framed his shoulders well and he was, of course, as handsome as always. They both had the clothes and they were at the location. Now, it was time to confront their opponents for the night.

"You look fine," he insisted and waved a hand airily. "You're worrying far too much. This won't end in some huge war or blood vendetta."

"It could end in a vendetta," she muttered.

"They aren't like that. I've already told you that. I know you don't believe me, but it's the truth."

Is this a little payback? Maybe. I can't blame him after what I put him through before.

No, no, no. I can't think that way. This will totally go great. There won't be any explosions or killing or weird Oriceran lizard-guys. I only have to go in and be honest and myself. Unless they hate honesty and they hate my normal personality.

Mason offered his arm, and Alison took it. They walked up the narrow cement path across the yard. A light dusting of snow coated the area, but her galloping heart would have kept her warm even without her coat. She would have rather kicked in a warehouse full of wizard assassins. At least, in that situation, she knew exactly how to handle herself.

She swallowed as they reached the front door. It was innocuous and a woven mat reading *WELCOME* rested in front, like bait for a trap.

You don't fool me. I know this won't be some happy chat.

"Why do I feel like I should have a shield and shadow blade ready?" she muttered. Her hands twitched, and she wondered if the witch and wizard inside would find it amusing if she stepped inside with her defenses ready.

Mason snickered. "These aren't people you need that kind of magic for, A. Calm down."

"Says you. But you're on their good side. Me? Maybe not."

A grin grew on his face. "I had to face this same situation. I even agreed to stay in the situation for several days. I went into the dragon's den, so you can, too."

He reached up to knock on the door but it swung open to reveal a smiling blonde woman in a light-blue dress and an apron. Her smooth face made her look like she was in her late thirties, even though Alison knew she was in her early fifties. Asking if it was good genes or life magic didn't strike her as polite, though, especially since the family resemblance to Mason was unmistakable.

"Hello, Mom," he said with a smile.

She pulled him into a tight embrace. "Considering we live in the same city, it's been far too long."

A slender near-clone of Mason with about ten extra

years on his face stepped behind the woman. Mason's father, Henry, seemed a little more imposing than her boyfriend, though.

Alison managed a smile, despite her every instinct telling her to run—or fly, because she could, come to think of it. "Hello, Dr. Lind, and...uh, Dr. Lind."

His mother, Carla, laughed. "No. That won't do. Call us Carla and Henry."

"Okay." She smiled. "Mason's told me so much about you."

At least this shouldn't open with them asking how many three-headed dragons I've killed.

Alison smiled at Carla as she finished another bite of roasted chicken. She couldn't claim it was the best she'd ever tasted, but it wasn't bad. The first twenty minutes of the meal had proceeded with very basic small talk. They'd even spent five minutes discussing the recent snow.

"I saw on the news that your team helped to escort those Shimmer Rays," Henry commented. "And you managed to capture the three poachers and turn them over to the authorities."

She nodded. "It was a straightforward job except that it involved the ocean."

Carla cleared her throat delicately. "Still, it's good whenever something like that can end without too much bloodshed."

Mason's jaw clenched.

Alison managed not to sigh.

Oh, I see. So it won't be, 'How many three-headed dragons have you killed?' but the opposite. He warned me they were very focused on healing, so I should have seen this coming.

She shrugged. "It is. I see the role of a security contractor in general as one of protection. Whenever I'm on a job and I encounter someone who intends violence to me or my team, I almost always try to give them a chance to walk away or surrender. Unfortunately, not everyone does, and I have to defend myself, my employees, and my clients."

"Oh, I understand that." Carla stared at her, her expression thoughtful. "As a doctor, you can imagine the kind of injuries I've had to treat, though. I'm not naïve to the full breadth and depth of intelligent species' ability and willingness to harm one another for the most thoughtless of reasons."

Henry nodded his agreement while he sipped his wine.

"When we do our job well," Mason interjected, "it leads to fewer people getting hurt."

His mother's gaze finally broke from Alison to drift to her son. "True, but if you'd followed the family tradition, you'd be a man helping to mend and not to break."

He frowned. "Mom, we've been over this before. Too many times. I'm not rehashing this argument now, especially in front of her." He nodded toward his girlfriend.

Alison grabbed her wine and gulped half of it. Honestly, she was too sober for this. Unlike Mason, she had basically followed in her family's violent, ass-kicking footsteps, although both her parents made it clear they wouldn't have stood in her way if she'd wanted a different career.

Carla leaned back in her chair and a slight frown

marred her face. "I don't mean to be rude. It's not like Alison's some woman you picked up at the gym or something. I understand that this is a serious relationship, so I see no reason to hold back."

She winced and didn't dare to correct the woman about where she had met her son.

"I'm happy I became a bodyguard," Mason insisted. "And I'm happy I joined Alison's company. Because of that, I've helped make this country and even the world a better place. We defeated Scott Carlyle together and ended his anti-magic plot. We helped stopped a dark wizard conspiracy stretching back decades, and that's not including all the rank-and-file criminal scum we've helped bring under control."

Henry grabbed a wine bottle to refill his glass. "Be careful, Mason. You don't want to let your job color your view of reality. Not everyone is scum."

"No, not everyone is scum." He shrugged. "Only the kind of people we often have to deal with. We're not talking some rival corporation that merely wants a few industrial secrets, but people who think nothing of killing children or trafficking."

Carla raised a hand. "I'm sorry. It was impolite. I shouldn't have brought it up. You're right. You decided to walk your own path a long time ago. That has little to do with Alison."

Alison finished off her second glass of wine and set it down. The warm cloud in her mind was welcome. She nodded slightly.

"So let's talk about things that do have to do with Alison," Carla continued.

"What are you talking about?" she squeaked and fixed the woman with a startled look.

"I'm interested in your plans for the future. After all, that's why you're here now, meeting us, isn't it? You're considering a future with Mason. So, let's talk about that."

She glanced at her boyfriend. He looked as confused as she felt, so she turned to his mother and waited for her to continue.

Carla shook her finger. "Come now. Neither of you is fresh out of high school and you're living together now, which means there's an eventual end-goal for this. I'm curious about whether you've thought about some of the implications."

"Implications, Mom?" he asked with a frown. He looked at his father, but the quiet man shrugged and hid behind a wine glass.

His mother nodded and turned toward Alison. "Have you talked about children yet?"

Mason opened his mouth to say something but closed it without uttering a word. He cast a curious glance at his girlfriend.

So, we're doing this, huh?

Alison looked at all three members of the Lind family before she shrugged. "To be honest, I've not really thought about it that much."

Carla's brow furrowed and a flicker of irritation crossed her face. "You've not thought about it?"

"I've thought about it a little, of course, and it's not like I have some huge objection to having children. That said, I'm not concerned about having any kids anytime soon. Everything I've heard suggests that my lifespan will likely be closer to a Drow's than a normal human, before taking any kind of magic into account." She laughed. "It's actually weird to even think about this when my mom's pregnant. So, my answer is, yes, I'm interested in kids, but I'm also not in any real hurry."

Henry nodded. Satisfaction filtered onto Mason's face, but she wasn't sure if he was happy about the idea that she wanted children or if he was merely happy that she had stood up to his mother.

"Well, that's a particularly unusual situation given that she's not your biological mother, from what I understand," Carla pointed out. "My point is that you are currently involved in a very dangerous line of work. If you do decide to have children, I can't see being a magical security contractor as a viable career path to promote family stability."

Alison wanted to blurt that it hadn't stopped her parents, but that wasn't true. James and Shay did keep their older jobs as a bounty hunter and tomb raider, respectively, for her first few years of high school. But by the time she graduated, they'd both all but retired to more stable and less dangerous careers. They didn't have to make the hard choice now that Shay was pregnant. They'd already made it.

"That may very well be true," she conceded. "But it's not as if it's a problem."

"Oh?" Carla raised an inquisitorial eyebrow. "How is it not a problem?"

"Because I have magic, a college degree, and millions of dollars." She shrugged. "I run a security company because I'm trying to make this city a better place in my own way, but it's not like I have to do that." She smiled at Mason. "For now, Mason and I want to use our abilities to help protect people. It's only a few decades since the gates began to open, after all. Everyone's still trying to work this all out. I'm sure that in a couple of decades, we won't need things like bounty hunters or security contractors to protect rare animals from wizards and Nerak."

"Are you sure you're not waiting too long, then?"

Mason snorted. "Come on, Mom."

Carla frowned. "What? It's a valid question."

"No, it's not. Not with a half-Drow and a life wizard." He gestured at both his parents. "Most people would assume you're my sister and dad my brother. Alison will live longer naturally, but everyone in our family lives longer because of magical techniques we've used in this family for a long time. It's not like if we don't pop out a grandchild for you in the next year, we won't ever have one."

The woman sniffed disdainfully. "I'm not saying anyone expects that. It merely might be nice if it happened sooner rather than in a couple of decades."

Alison took another sip of wine before she picked her fork up. She still had half a chicken breast to finish. It was a good excuse as any for hiding from the conversation.

"That's what this is really about, isn't it?" Mason smirked. "It's not so much about our plans but about your empty nest syndrome."

Carla's cheeks reddened, and she snatched her fork up to apply it to her own meal. Alison smiled around her mouthful.

A kid, huh? When I used the wish, they implied that another

31

wish might come when I had a daughter, but Rasila and Myna both also suggested that it isn't guaranteed for my line. Am I giving up the wish by not getting involved in Drow politics? Do I even care?

She took another bite of her chicken. Getting into Drow succession discussions might be a valid discussion for the future, but it wasn't a subject she wanted to discuss with Mason's parents.

"This is good chicken, by the way," she ventured. "You'll have to give me the recipe."

Carla beamed. "I'm glad you like it. All natural, not a single spell used."

Sometimes, a little ass-kissing is all you need.

CHAPTER FOUR

Alison smiled from the driver's seat of her Fiat. She and Mason had finished the dinner about twenty minutes prior and were on the way back home. They'd chatted about a funny story Carla shared concerning how reluctant patients could be both amusing and annoying at the same time.

That wasn't so bad, really. Not so bad at all. It could have been so much worse.

"Okay, I admit it," she admitted with a chuckle. "I was wrong, and you were right."

He glanced at her. "I'm happy to hear that, but what are you admitting you were wrong about? We didn't disagree at all about anything we just talked about unless you were having a very different conversation than I was. I wouldn't be surprised. Sometimes, I don't know what's going through your head."

"I thought meeting your parents would be this awful, painful thing, and I admit, it was awkward in the beginning. But once we got that out of the way, it really wasn't

33

so bad. I wouldn't exactly take your mom dancing with the girls, but she's all right, and I think we'll be friends." She snickered. "And I hope she doesn't get offended someday if she learns I didn't love her chicken recipe as much as I claimed. I confess, though, I'm still not sure about your dad. He didn't say much."

"Yeah, he's always been a man of few words. After a while, you learn to read what he's thinking from the expressions on his face." Mason shrugged. "And Mom's always been a woman of many words, so they balance each other out. It's kind of like with your parents."

Alison laughed. "You're right. Does your dad obsess over something like barbecue, too? Your mom spent all that time talking about cooking. At least we have that in common."

"Obsess? That might be too strong a word, but he likes golf."

She sighed. "My dad hates golf."

He nodded wryly. "I know. He mentioned it when he told me all those stories about his road trip during Christmas. I think he said, 'I fucking hate golf,' about six times when he talked about confronting those guys on the golf course."

A slight crease of concern pulled her brow as she glanced quickly at him. "I know I asked you this before, but I wanted to make sure. My dad didn't threaten you when I wasn't around, did he? If he did, I'll call him right now to chew him out. You don't have to put up with that crap simply because he's James Brownstone."

"Nope. If anything, it was the opposite." Mason grimaced. "It was kind of creepy, actually."

"Creepy?" She checked the mirror and camera before changing lanes. "What was creepy?"

"Your dad." He shrugged. "He was almost jolly. Well, as jolly as he gets, anyway. Like Santa Claus with tattoos. I told you before we went there that I was worried his newfound respect for me wouldn't last, but I didn't have a problem at all. I think the old lady who lives across the street gave me more dirty looks than your dad."

"That makes sense," Alison replied and nodded, satisfied. She'd thought the Christmas visit to her parents had gone well, but she had still harbored some small doubt that Mason was merely trying to protect her from her dad's intolerance.

"Really? That makes sense?" Mason asked. "Is he that into Christmas or something?"

"No. I mean he always goes to Christmas Mass, but I don't know if he thinks it's all that fun." She shrugged. "Necessary is probably closer to the truth."

He frowned. "I'm confused, then. Why does it make sense? I'll be honest, A. There's nothing you've ever told me in all our time together that makes it seem like your dad's a jolly guy, even when cooking barbecue."

"You already mentioned the reason indirectly." Alison grinned. "His road trip. It reset everything."

"Reset everything?"

"Yeah. His head was basically up his ass about having a new kid, especially when he'd resigned himself to the idea I would be his only kid. He'd gotten used to a very particular lifestyle."

Mason chuckled. "And he thought a new baby would cramp his style?"

She shook her head. "It's not like that. You have to understand that he grew up in an orphanage and he's suffered many losses. With me, I was already almost an adult and he was worried that he wouldn't be able to do a good job despite both Mom and I telling him not to worry."

He considered that for a moment before he responded. "But going on a barbecue road trip and kicking some ass along the way convinced him he will do a good job?"

Alison chucked. "It sounds weird when you say it that way. I think it gave him time to think, and honestly, to relax a little. Sometimes, you have to simply let a Brownstone be a Brownstone."

"Don't I know it."

"He was able to visit with old friends, kick ass, and protect the one thing in existence he cares about almost as much as his family and God."

"Barbecue?" he replied, a smirk on his face.

"Exactly, barbecue." She slowed to a stop at a red light. "He gets in his head because even after all these years, he's not comfortable with talking about his feelings with Mom or me. Sometimes, getting out there and kicking a few assholes around helps him to come to terms with it. It's almost like it's meditation for him."

I wish it worked that way for me.

"Punching a guy is meditation?" Mason laughed. "I must be doing it wrong. I don't feel any closer to enlightenment." He shook his head. "Okay, whatever works. I'm not complaining. He wasn't rude to me during my visit, and he didn't seem ready to challenge me to a duel. We didn't exactly have the deepest conversations, but he did like stories about my jobs with you or before. The funny thing is, he didn't seem to care all that much about sharing most of his own stories besides the stuff from the road trip whereas before, he constantly tried to talk up all the tough monsters and guys he'd taken out."

"Yeah, you only have to understand the way Dad's mind works. He never wanted fame or money. In his mind, God made him a tough guy, so that's the kind of work he fell into. He hates fame and people always wanting autographs and that kind of thing. He used to be interested in talking himself up only because it was a useful way to intimidate bounties. That's why he boasted about all those things before. It was a weapon to use against someone he considered a threat, and now he no longer considers you a threat, he doesn't feel a need to mention every three-headed dragon or chaos demon he's killed."

He nodded slowly as he took it all in. "That's a good thing, I think."

"Now that he's a pitmaster rather than a bounty hunter —at least most days of the year—he cares even less," Alison replied. "I think in his perfect world, everyone would forget that James Brownstone was a bounty hunter and focus on his food. Not him, but his food."

The light changed, and she pulled forward.

"I think that's more of a distant dream than world peace," Mason replied. "Given everything your dad has done, I think it'll be a long time before people stop thinking of him as anything other than the Granite Ghost or the Scourge of Harriken." He shrugged. "I wonder if everything would have been worse if I were a doctor or healer. He might not have been able to relate to me at all, but then you wouldn't have had to deal with an inquisition from my mother about your future plans for children and how your career might impact that. I'm still sorry about that. I don't think telling you that Mom can be pushy was enough to prepare you for that level of bluntness."

"It wasn't that bad. It merely caught me off-guard." She licked her lips and focused her gaze on the road, although she was tempted to glance at his face to try to read it. "Are you mad that I didn't have a clearer answer about kids? I was honest, but I understand that it might come off as a dodge."

Small snowflakes began to drift to the ground. She turned the wipers on. The roads were mostly clear, the result of a combination of plows and contracted magical specialists.

Mason shook his head. "It's not like you said absolutely not, but I won't sit here and pretend I don't think a lot more about that kind of thing in the future. My mom's right about stable environments, and you're right about both of us still having time to think about it. That's one of the many advantages of being a magical."

Alison blew a breath out. "Even though nobody used the word tonight, I want to be clear on what we're talking about."

"Sure."

"Marriage, right? That's what we're talking about. It's the next logical step."

He grinned. "Logic. Ouch, A. We have a relationship built on, I hope, mutual love, respect, and understanding and not merely logical steps."

She sighed. "I didn't mean it to come out that way. I

only want to be one hundred percent clear on what we're talking about."

"Yes. I'd say then, in that case, it's the next logical step." He sent her a lop-sided grin. "Is that so crazy?"

"I'm not saying it's crazy. It's only…whoa, marriage. It's a big deal—the actual commitment."

"I know." He looked ahead and his expression turned serious. "And I understand that we only moved in together not all that long ago. I can't even say I'm totally ready. For one thing, women deserve a proper proposal, and there was one epic tale your father reinforced to me during Christmas that I didn't tell you about."

Oh no. Dad, tell me you didn't.

Alison sighed. "What was that?"

He laughed. "About how he was ready to marry your mother, but she stopped him and demanded—how did he put it?—a fucking epic proposal, so he wracked his brain until a situation presented itself."

She forced herself not to stare at him. Her father's epic proposal had involved, among other things, the military and an alien spaceship. The truth of his extraterrestrial nature was something she had kept from him, and only a few of her friends from before her time in Seattle knew the truth.

Did Dad actually tell him?

"Oh?" she asked and feigned an innocent tone. "Did he tell you about what he did?"

"No. He only said, 'The opportunity presented itself.'" He frowned a little as if he'd suddenly realized something. "Now that you mention it, that's kind of weird. What did happen exactly?"

Alison shook her head. "I…can't really talk about it, not without his permission. It was a special thing, and it's not for me to share."

"Fair enough," Mason replied.

Sloppy, Dad. Why would you lay the seed there unless…do you want me to tell him? No, I won't do that until I have your explicit permission.

They fell into silence for a couple of minutes, Alison lost in the thoughts of the past and the potential future.

"I'm not saying I'm ready for anything right away," she explained a short while later. "But I want to make something very clear. I love Mom, but I'm not her. When you feel the time is right, I'm not looking for a fucking epic proposal. I only want something that feels right for both of us. A surprise would be nice, too."

"You went from no conditions to a list of conditions," he noted with a smirk.

"Sure, but those aren't terribly difficult conditions to meet."

"I'll keep that in mind."

CHAPTER FIVE

A couple of days later, Alison settled in behind her desk and stretched, a slight smile on her face. Both her main magical team and Jerry's team wouldn't work any jobs for a few days. Sometimes, she liked to let the company have a week or two to breathe—not a true vacation, merely time to train and relax between lizardmen poachers and corporate assassins, let alone crazy potions of mass destruction.

She had asked Ava to deflect major jobs for the next week or two, subject to the administrative assistant's personal judgment. The Englishwoman was often better at understanding what was best for the company than even the boss was.

"I might as well get this over with." She scowled at her phone. After her conversation with Mason on the weekend, there was something she wanted to confirm and a simple phone call should accomplish that. Rather than waste any more time worrying about it, she dialed her father.

"Is something wrong?" James answered with a rumble.

"No." She laughed. "I really need to call you more often simply to chat so you don't always think there's trouble."

"It's not that. But, you know, a lot of shit's happened over the last couple of months—to both of us. Brownstone luck."

"I thought I'd let you know I met Mason's parents last Saturday," Alison explained. "You're partially responsible for pushing things this way, so I thought I'd talk to you about it first, rather than Mom."

"Good." He grunted. "Were they assholes? There's no law that says you have to like your boyfriend's parents."

"Easy for you to say, considering Mom would probably shoot her parents if she saw them." She laughed. "And, no, they weren't assholes. Not really. I don't think we'll be best friends or anything, but they don't seem to have much against me, other than some mild concern about my rough line of work. They were more interested in things like kids."

"Kids?" He scoffed. "It'll be a while. You're barely out of school."

"Well, sure, it'll be a while, but I'm not *barely* out of school. Sometimes, I still think—"

"That I see you as that teenage girl who brought me my missing dog," James completed. "Yeah, yeah. Just saying."

"Anyway, I did say I didn't envision me having kids for a while." She exhaled a satisfied sigh. "But the point is, it went off fine for the most part, and I wanted to make sure you and Mom knew about it. I let it sit for a few days in case they were only pretending to be nice, but everything seems stable. I don't have much else I wanted to tell you, so

I'll let you go. I know how much you hate chitchatting on the phone."

"Wait," he said quickly.

She straightened and her heart now pounded as she worried her father wasn't as satisfied with Mason as she believed. "What?"

"I was curious about something. I was talking to Trey the other day, and he mentioned how their Ultimate problems in Vegas have mostly gone away since we did our thing during my road trip."

The drug Ultimate could be used to enhance magical power, but heavy side-effects accompanied its usage, including potential physical and mental transformations. It'd appeared on the underworld's radar in the last several months. Various clues had pointed to Texas initially, but the government still struggled for viable intel. Its source remained unknown, with PDA, DEA, and FBI investigations dead-ending at the basic suppliers. Some people suspected a foreign plot, either Oriceran or Earth-based.

"That's good to hear," Alison replied. "I doubted it would spread into LA because of you, but it's great that you guys cut it off in Vegas. The last thing this country needs is some weird magic-enhancing drug that messes with people."

"Have you seen any up there?" James asked with something approaching concern in the grinding bass of his voice.

"Of all the strange things I've had to deal with in the last six months, Ultimate hasn't been one of them, and I have solid underworld and law enforcement contacts up here." She chuckled. "Tahir also has all kinds of special things crawling around the net looking for trouble. If there was Ultimate being used or dealt, I think I'd know. Why do you ask?"

"No big reason." He grunted. "I only want to make sure you don't have extra bullshit to deal with. I know things are a lot easier than when you first moved up there, but now you have those Drow sniffing around, too. I hoped that dealing with the fucking dark wizards would have made it vacation time for you, but it's not like anyone wants to let you rest."

"The Drow situation is under control," she explained. "I've met with Rasila several times, at least, and she's not interested in taking another shot at me, and..." She sighed. "I don't know how to explain it. We're not friends, but she's very interested in gaining my support one way or another, so she's done a lot to keep me aware of Drow movements and help me."

"And you're sure she's not playing you?"

Alison laughed. "I assume so."

"Huh?"

"I assume she's playing me on some level. I won't force her under truth spells every time because it'd be insulting, and I think she's well past the point where she would directly lie to me. But don't get me wrong. I understand that any help she gives me is provided because she thinks she'll get something out of it long-term, whether it's her as the new queen or even some weird situation where I'm the new queen dispensing favors to her."

"I'm the last man to suggest something like this, but have you thought about reaching out to the other princesses? Diplomacy shit and all that?" James almost growled the last sentence.

Alison sighed. "Yeah, I have, but I'd rather not. The more involved I get with the Drow princesses, the more swept up I'll be in all this stuff. So far, the only person who has attacked me is Rasila. Maybe the fact that I didn't storm over to Oriceran after that might help convince the others I'm not all that interested in being queen and keep them from messing with me."

"If you need my help, ask. I don't give a shit about who becomes Drow queen, but if you need me to beat someone down, I will. It's not like I haven't done it before."

She snorted. "That's not even an option. No offense, Dad, but I think the last thing the Drow need right now is you getting involved again. Don't worry about it. If they try anything again, I'll take care of it. If we're lucky, no one will bother me for years."

He scoffed. "Brownstones aren't that lucky."

<hr />

Sonya yawned loudly as she tapped her keyboard. She'd spent most of the day at Brownstone Security helping Tahir reinforce some of the system defenses and most of the night exploring some of the new battle drone race-courses. Her day job kept her from putting as much time into her hobby as she would have liked, but it wasn't like she would complain to Tahir and Alison about giving her a well-paying job and a free apprenticeship because she wanted to play more. Occasionally, she thought about becoming a pro racer, but that seemed silly given all her other talents and training.

The girl might not always show it, but she woke up every day grateful for the luck that brought Tahir, Hana, and Alison into her life. When she had lived alone, she'd thought she was satisfied. Or, more accurately, she'd convinced herself of that.

She had believed she didn't need anyone, let alone the father who had abandoned her to her abusive mother. That mindset had simply ignored all the times she went to sleep in the old empty apartment alone, a void in her soul. She might not be comfortable around people, but she still needed them.

An alert popped up on her screen and she frowned. She leaned forward. It was an old honeypot she'd set up on servers she used to tinker with when she still lived in the apartment. Since she'd moved in with Alison and started at Brownstone Security, Tahir had provided her with new servers and systems to practice her hacking and infomancy skills—servers he'd hardened himself. She'd maintained the older systems mostly out of nostalgia.

Who would care about hacking her old systems? There had never been anything of value there.

Sonya's wand remained slotted into her keyboard, which allowed her magic if she needed it, but pride fueled a conventional attempt. Using infomancy against a non-magical hacker was an admission of inferiority, and while she still had a long way to go, she was far better than her age might suggest.

Her mouth curled into a grin as her fingers danced across the keyboard. "Whoever you are, I'll give you credit. You couldn't have found that server merely by scanning at random. I made a mistake somewhere and you probably followed it, but now, it's nothing but a trap for fools."

Behind a keyboard, all the fear, worry, and uncertainty that seemed to define her melted away. Confidence filled her soul, and she never felt the need to withdraw into herself. She might still be figuring out where she fit in the real world, but online, she was as much as a warrior princess as Alison.

"Seriously?" Sonya rolled her eyes. "You are so lame. I can't believe you've fallen for such an obvious trap." She entered a few commands. It was time to trace the attacker and launch a counterattack. Nothing serious, of course, simply a little poke in the eye—a hacker's way to say hello and show them who they had messed with.

A huge smirk took over her face as she continued to track her opponent. They weren't a total loser. The trail led her through proxy servers all over the world. This probably wasn't some script kiddy sitting in their room. Then again, she was a kid sitting in her room.

"You're not getting—"

Sonya narrowed her eyes and gritted her teeth. The trace became erratic and jumped randomly with each individual node identified. She'd seen this before, as she'd used the exact defense on display herself.

"Another infomancer," she muttered, then snorted. "Fine, man. If you want to go magic, let's go magic. I'll pants you and then you'll be sorry." She clicked her mouse on a series of stored enchantment scripts and her grin returned. Her mentor was one of the best infomancers in the country. There was no way some random fool on the net would win against her.

A window popped up, filled with glyphs. She closed her eyes and whispered a few additional incantations. Tahir could rely almost entirely on the incantation scripts, but she still needed to master several magical energy conservation techniques before she could successfully accomplish the same trick for every spell.

Her trace stabilized and accelerated, and the jump from proxy to proxy now became more reasonable.

"I have you, man." Sonya laughed. "I'm about to own you. If only you knew who was doing it to you, you would be so embarrassed, but it's not like I'm stupid enough to send a picture."

Several alarm windows appeared. Her opponent now attempted something very similar. She snorted and executed another spell script. This one tried to deceive in a more subtle way. She wanted to lead her opponent to a dead-end at the Department of Defense, which might garner him a little extra attention and scare him. People shouldn't fool around with hacking if they weren't prepared for the occasional angry government agent knocking on their door.

Her smile faded. A bar in the corner of her screen filled slowly with white. The monitoring spell helped her determine how close an infomancy-based trace might be to reaching her system. She had no idea if the other infomancer attempted a more direct scrying spell but didn't worry about it at all. Alison had so many wards on her house that King Oriceran himself probably couldn't peer inside without difficulty.

"You won't win against me, man. So give it up." Sonya entered a few additional commands before she cast another spell to reinforce her trace from a different direction. Sweat beaded on her forehead. The mental and magical concentration proved taxing. "Tahir would have already found your lame ass and defeated you, but I'll still win this. Wait and see. My multiplex filter is something you've probably never even seen." She snorted. "This won't end with a poke, now. I'll have to bloody your nose a little for being so stubborn."

Her monitoring bar suddenly filled up to the top.

"What the?" Her eyes widened. "No way." She hastily entered a command to sever her connection. Sometimes, she lost and that was embarrassing, but sticking around to have her butt kicked even harder was where things became stupid.

The computer screen turned black, and her heart pounded. Her breathing turned ragged, and she wondered if she should tell Alison. After all, the infomancer might not have complete access to the home, but he had successfully traced her to the location. Then again, it wasn't as if Alison's address was a national secret.

The girl swallowed as a single letter popped up on the screen: **I**.

A few deep breaths later, she nibbled on her lip and typed her response.

I what?

I'm not your enemy.

She snorted.

You're breaking into my system, man. Maybe you're not my enemy, but that's rude.

You didn't lock the doors properly, the hacker responded. **Is it really so bad I decided to check what's inside?**

Sonya narrowed her eyes.

Screw you, man.

That doesn't change the truth.

It was almost too tempting to type out, "Do you know who I work for?" but she stopped herself. This wasn't Brownstone Security business. She'd screwed up and let some punk infomancer breach her defenses and trace her. It was her mess, and she needed to clean it up.

You got lucky, she responded. **Don't let it go to your head. I'll beat your ass next time, man.**

Do you remember the giraffe you used to love? You won it in a claw machine at the beach when you were seven years old. You used to love that giraffe. You slept with it every night until you lost it. Left it behind at a restaurant. Your father wanted to go back for it, but your mother said no. She said you needed to learn a lesson about taking care of your things, and by the time he did go back to check on it, they'd already given it away.

She swallowed, her heart now thundering.

How do you know that? she responded. **Who are you?**

A friend. If you're interested in learning more, you can send an encrypted message to the following address. But for now, I'm going. You might not be who I think you are, and we both need to be careful.

Sonya stared at the address and shook her head. A moment later, she noticed her various monitoring spells indicated that they were no longer connected. She stood slowly and backed away from her computer until she fell onto her bed.

The hacker's anecdote had been true, as far as she could remember. She did have a stuffed giraffe she loved and had named him Gino. The loss of the toy was one of the first times in life when she understood what it could feel like to lose something or someone you cared about, but she only vaguely remembered her parents discussing it. Mostly, she remembered the crying.

She took several deep breaths as she tried to bring her heart under control. No one knew about that giraffe. She slept with it at home but she never talked about it at school. For some reason, she'd convinced herself that if any of the other kids knew about Gino, they'd steal him. She'd even half-convinced herself that one of those kids went to the restaurant and claimed the toy was his.

Only two people knew about that giraffe—her mother and father—and only one of them had any real possibility of being alive.

The girl sat up and stared at her computer. Her father was an infomancer. He'd always been halfway decent, but her mother's disdain for magic had kept him from training her too much, and there was only so much he could accomplish before her magic manifested.

Sonya had assumed he was dead. He'd not always interacted with the nicest of people. The idea of some mobster killing him after he'd crossed him in some way was far too plausible. She wasn't even sure how surprised or saddened she had been when he had disappeared, rather than being resigned to the near-certain inevitability of such an end. There was only so much pity she could spare for him.

She'd been left behind to suffer at the hands of her mother, after all.

"He could have told someone else the story," she whispered. "Or Mom did, and they're using it to get to me. They probably don't even care about me. This is probably someone trying to get to Alison." She rolled onto her side. "Maybe I should tell her, but if this is only Dad, maybe I should take care of everything myself. Alison, Tahir, and Hana have already done a lot for me. They shouldn't have to worry about my messed-up family."

She groaned, grabbed her pillow, and clutched it tightly against her chest. The corners of her eyes glistened.

Her old life was supposed to be dead and buried. She lived with the Dark Princess now and was trained by Tahir. Even if she didn't know for certain where her future would take her, it was supposed to be far away from the old apartment and the dark memories of two people who didn't deserve to be called parents.

Tears seeped from her eyes.

"It's not fair," she sobbed. "It's not fair."

CHAPTER SIX

Tahir looked over his shoulder and away from his three screens toward Sonya, who sat at her workstation. The girl wasn't social on the best of days, but her behavior that entire morning bordered on sulking, her movements slow and even her typing ponderous. While he would never claim to be a brilliant discerner of the true thoughts of the average person, he'd spent enough time with Sonya and Hana to understand their general moods and body language. Something was clearly wrong, and he was duty-bound to help the girl—or, at least, to make some kind of attempt to do so.

"You should simply tell me what's bothering you," he suggested. "If you're not in optimal mental condition, it'll negatively impact your training. That's wasting not only your time but also mine. There are few things I despise more than wasting my time."

"Sorry." She sighed and turned her chair to face him. "I'm fairly sure my dad is alive, and it's messing with my head, man."

"Alive?" He frowned. "Really now? And what do you base this conclusion on? To the best of my knowledge, you haven't attempted to trace his whereabouts. I thought you were satisfied with the situation."

"I am." Sonya shrugged. "And no. I didn't go looking for him. I think I never wanted to know one way or another. But if it is him, he forced the issue."

"How so?"

"Someone hacked into my old servers the other night," she explained. "I messed around with them, but they ended up tracing me."

The infomancer scoffed. "I've taught you better than that."

"I know." She rolled her eyes. "Give me a break. We chatted a little, and at the end, the hacker told a story that only my parents knew about. They sent me an address for future messages, too, but I don't know how to handle it. I have mixed feelings and all that crap. I wasn't sure if he was alive or dead, and now, he suddenly comes out of nowhere. Part of me says he left me with that shrew, and that meant he left me to get beaten, and the other part says maybe he had no choice." She shrugged. "Maybe I should meet him to tell him to go throw himself in the bay—assuming it is him."

Tahir nodded slowly. "I see. I will note one thing that might seem strange to you since you're still so young. Your life will be a series of both triumphs and disappointments. Such an existence is inevitable for all people of talent, but one important way to move on from the disappointments is to achieve closure. Regret saps the will and leads to wasted time. A focus on self-improvement and the future is what transforms a mediocre person with potential into someone actualizing their talents into reality."

Sonya blinked. "Wow. I didn't expect you to say that."

"What is that?"

"I thought you'd say, 'Ignore him.'" Sonya shrugged.

"Some things are easier to ignore than others," he countered.

"So you think I should try to meet him? I assumed you would tell me it's all some complicated plot to screw Alison over or frame me so the mob comes after me instead of him or something. Or that it might not even be him." Sonya sighed. "By the way, I checked a few other things. There were some code signatures I was able to nab that remind me of my dad, but it's not like that can't be faked."

"I'm dubious that it's some overly complicated plot, if only because finding a particular anecdote to convince you would be an unlikely turn of events." Tahir chuckled. "That said, a healthy suspicion is always warranted, both in our line of work and given who our employer is. Still, I'm more concerned about your long-term mental health than mini-mizing dangers from third-rate threats to Alison. If she can win against a Drow princess or a government super-soldier, I doubt your father has access to anyone who could dream of posing a threat to her.

"I'm also dubious that any true threat to her would rely on such an unreliable attack vector as an apprentice info-mancer. I don't say this to demean you but to provide a realistic appraisal from my perspective of the likely threats. This is, based on what you say, most likely your father. He might present a threat of some sort, but everything you've told me suggests he can be handled if that is the case." He shrugged. "So worry about your choice and how it benefits you. All other considerations should be secondary in this particular situation."

"Okay, then." She nodded, a slightly incredulous expression on her face. "Maybe I will meet him. To get...uh, closure like you said." She looked pained. "If this is some lame attempt of his to swoop in and try to be my father again, I'll simply spit in his face. Maybe he feels bad now or wants his family back."

"It's a distinct possibility, and while I think it's your choice, I will note that those who don't plan for negative outcomes suffer the most if they come." The infomancer frowned. "Thus, I do think you should take that into account in your decision-making process."

Sonya frowned a little as she thought about this. "I don't get it. Do you think I should meet him or don't you? You're sending mixed signals."

"Let me clarify. I think only you can make the choice about whether or not to try to meet him, but if you do choose to do so, meeting him alone would be beyond foolish. You lack the physical or magical capabilities to defend yourself properly." Tahir shook his head. "And I can't allow any apprentice of mine to embarrass me by doing something foolish."

"I don't get it."

"It's simple." He gave her a thin smile. "If you choose to meet him, you'll have backup. You think about what you want to do, and I'll handle the rest."

Her eyes widened. "Oh. Is it okay if I take a while to decide?"

"Of course. It's your father and your choice."

Hana bolted out of her chair at the conference room table when Tahir finished explaining the situation. "Absolutely fucking no way," she declared, her tone almost a growl.

For now, this was less a Brownstone Security matter than a personal family matter, so Alison didn't see the need to involve either Ava or Jerry in the conversation yet. Personal errands had taken both Mason and Drysi away from the building, but she would bring them up to speed later.

It wouldn't have been surprising if her friend foxed out right there and shredded the table. It was rare to see her so angry, but then again, it was rare to encounter a potential threat against someone Hana had begun to see as, if not a daughter, then at least a younger sister. Sonya might live with Alison, but she spent considerable time around Hana and Tahir.

The fox had lost her family due to terrorism and found a new one at Brownstone Security. Alison didn't always appreciate how important that was, and she strived to remember it. She had a loving father and mother and friends she cared about from school. Hana had lived a life not trusting anyone and had only learned in the last year to put others before herself. A burning desire to defend the girl wasn't strange, even if it was inconvenient in the current conversation.

"Let's keep calm, Hana," she suggested. "Losing it won't help us figure out the best way to handle the situation."

Tahir sat beside Hana, his expression bland and neutral.

He nodded slightly at his boss' suggestion but appeared content to let her talk his girlfriend down.

Hana pounded her fist on the desk. "I can't believe we're even considering it. This asshole loser left his own daughter behind. Screw him. I can't believe he has the balls to try to show his face to her again. He's not the worst parent of the two, but only because her mother was an abusive bitch. That doesn't make him a good guy who deserves to be in her life."

"We don't know what precipitated his choice to leave her behind," the infomancer replied with a shrug. "It might have been necessary for the safety of his family. We shouldn't presume too much and assign him villainy when he might be a hero."

"Hero?" She snorted

"I've simply presented it as a possibility."

She dropped into her seat and folded her arms. "You know what's not safe? Leaving your daughter to be whaled on by your angry wife who hates her magic."

"Maybe he didn't know his wife would be like that when he left," Alison suggested. "Maybe he believed they would come together and be stronger in his absence." She wanted to believe the words even though they rang hollow as she said them.

"No offense, but I think even you know that's absolute bullshit." The fox shook her head. "There's no way that guy was married to Sonya's mother for as long as he had been without knowing her feelings or how she would react when he left. If this was about protecting Sonya, he could have disappeared and made arrangements for her to be taken care of by someone who actually loved her and wouldn't abuse her. I don't care if he feels bad about it now —and that's assuming he does. I say too damned late. I will admit one thing, though."

"What's that?"

She grinned, and the expression turned vicious and predatory. "I really, really would like to meet him."

"Oh?" Tahir asked. "I'm afraid to ask, but I feel I must. Why?"

"Because I'd like to introduce him to my claws or my sword. Or, at least, simply kick him really hard in the balls. Although given the way he abandoned his own daughter, he probably doesn't have any."

Alison shook her head. "I'm sympathetic. I'm very sympathetic, but we don't know the exact situation, so we can't make any plans without any real information."

Am I being a hypocrite here? I know how I wanted my biological dad handled, but that wasn't the same situation. It certainly gave me closure, though, and I don't regret what happened to him at all.

Or is it the same? He wanted to hand me over to criminals whom he knew would hurt me if not kill me. If Sonya's dad even suspected her mom would do the same when he left, he's at fault too.

Hana scoffed. "You think dickwad worst dad of the year will threaten us with a lawyer or something? I'd like to see him try."

"No, it has nothing to do with that." Alison gestured toward Tahir. "He gave Sonya the right advice. This is her life and her dad—or, at least, most likely her dad. We'll back her up regardless of what she chooses, but we have to grant her the respect to make the actual choice herself. We don't want her to spend the rest of her life wondering about what might have been because we forced her hand one way or another. We're supposed to mentor her, and part of that is helping her learn responsibility."

The other woman took a few deep breaths and finally gave a shallow nod. "Whatever. If he is trying some kind of stunt, he'll regret ever getting close to her. I promise you that." She shrugged. "I'm not saying I'll kill him, but I'll definitely put the fear of the fox into him."

Alison nodded. "I think we're all in agreement on that." She glanced at Tahir. "Right?"

The informancer nodded agreement. "I'll tell her to take her time, and we'll help her once she's decided."

CHAPTER SEVEN

Sonya's breaths emerged in puffs. The noonday sun wasn't enough to keep the winter chill of January away. She rubbed her wool-gloved hands together as she waited on the cold metal park bench. She'd sent a message to the address requesting a meeting at noon at the park on Tahir's advice. Everyone wanted somewhere reasonably public but not too public in case a fight broke out.

There wasn't anyone else near her at the moment with the exception of Alison, Mason, and Hana hidden among the trees nearby. Drysi had offered to help, which surprised Sonya as she didn't know the Welsh witch that well and didn't talk to her all that much, but their boss demurred. She'd felt they didn't need that much power yet.

The woman seemed disappointed, but from what the girl could tell, that was more about her wanting to be part of a good dust-up than because she was all that concerned about their youngest team member. The girl wasn't offended. Everyone had their reasons for what they did, and some were less noble than others.

A single dark drone circled high overhead. It was controlled by Tahir and a closer inspection might reveal the stun cannon mounted on the bottom.

Against the infomancer's advice, she asked to have the meeting without a receiver. She wanted to talk to her father without being distracted, and with the team watching her so closely, it wasn't like she needed to tell them if she landed in trouble.

Everyone told her constantly that it was her choice, so she chose to believe them. This meeting might be the beginning of re-establishing her old family or it might mark the beginning of the end of her old life. She honestly couldn't say which she preferred.

It had been so easy to hate her father, but the chance that they could be together again sapped the anger. She'd always gotten along well with him, and he'd been the one to help teach her when her magic came in. The memories of good times mingled with the frustration in her heart, which made it difficult to dismiss him entirely, no matter what Hana had to say.

A man in a long gray winter coat walked toward her and his boots thudded against the pavement. Sonya held her breath as he moved closer and his features resolved into clearer detail. The face was the same, even if he now sported a dirty blond beard. It was her father, Clayton.

She swallowed and rubbed her hands together. Her stomach clenched. Maybe the whole idea was stupid and she should never have sent him a message. It didn't matter and it was too late to run. He had already seen her.

It took him a minute to walk down the path and closer to the bench. He stood a few yards away from her, uncertainty on his face and his hands in his pockets. He waited in silence and watched his daughter warily.

"You won't get a hug if that's what you're waiting for," she commented. "At a minimum, you owe me for years of child support, you deadbeat. I might not want you dead, but that doesn't mean I'm happy to see you."

He nodded, resignation on his face. "I hoped for a hug but didn't expect one." He glanced up. "Is that your drone? Or do you have someone watching you? I've heard a lot of things about where you ended up, and when I checked around, those rumors seemed to be true, but you never know."

"I have a number of people watching me, yeah. So if this is some kind of trap, you'll end up with a shadow blade at your throat." Sonya narrowed her eyes. "And you're already supposed to be dead, so it's not like Seattle will miss a dead guy."

Her father stared at her, his gaze searching and his eyes despondent. "If you had to end up with someone, I suppose the Dark Princess isn't a bad choice. At least it means you're safe and well taken care of."

She scoffed. "Is this the part where you justify running away and leaving me with Mom because I ended up somewhere nice in the end? I was alone for a while before that, and that's not even taking into account what Mom did to me."

Clayton averted his gaze. "I...knew there might be issues. I hoped there wouldn't be, but—"

Sonya leapt off the bench, trembling with rage. "You *hoped* there wouldn't be? You left me. I wasn't even sure if you were alive, and all you do is show up and say, 'Hey, sorry your mom beat you and I was nowhere to be found. Stuff happens.' You think I'd buy that, man? Screw you. You don't get any credit from me for running like you did. You're a coward and a bad father."

"You have to understand." He took a deep breath. "At the time, I had no choice but to leave. It tore me up, but it was the only option."

She sneered. "Let me guess. You got mixed up with some bad men, and they were going to kill you. That story makes the most sense, I suppose, because you always did want to reach farther than your skills would take you."

"Yeah, basically." The man chuckled as embarrassment and cold reddened his face. "Very bad men. The 'I'll torture you first to make an example of you' kind of bad men—or at least one. A guy named Pista Varga, really nasty. Mostly operates out of Central Europe, but he has some connections here. He thinks of himself as an export-import guy, but he's into other nasty stuff—trafficking, arms dealing, drugs. You name it. If it turns your stomach, he's probably making a percentage off it."

"Okay, so what?" she shrugged. "I'm supposed to forgive everything because you let some terrible waste of skin pay you money to help him and you managed to piss him off? It's not your fault you're stupid, Dad."

Clayton rubbed his temples. "Sonya, you don't understand. That's not the situation."

Sonya threw her hands up. "Then explain to me and make it quick, because it's cold out here and I want to go back inside to somewhere warm and that doesn't stink so much of failure and loserdom."

"I deserve that. I deserve everything you've said." He

sighed. "But the thing is, I thought Varga might go after you, so I decided if I ran, it'd take the heat off you. I thought he would look for me, and he did, right? He never came after you even before you worked for the Dark Princess."

"Your brilliant logic was this scumbag might go after your kid, so you left her alone with someone who hated her for what she was? Forgive me if I'm not overwhelmed by your brilliance, Dad. It really sounds like you simply ran off without any thought about what might happen to me. I didn't even know if you were still alive."

"I had to be careful. I had to fall off the grid and keep moving. I—"

"Please, shut up with the excuses already," she screamed. "I, I, I. That's what it comes down to, doesn't it? *You* had to protect yourself and screw the rest of us. It was only 'good luck and see you around.'"

Anger heated her entire body. She had difficulty looking most people in the eye, but the fire inside helped her lock gazes with her returned father. More than anything, she wanted him to understand her pain. He needed to understand what he'd put her through.

"Look, I get that I screwed up in a lot of ways," Clayton responded. "I can't deny that, but I realized with everything you've told me that the best place for me was at your side. The problem is, I can't be at your side, not without some help."

"What do you mean?"

He sighed. "Varga's not done with me. I thought if I laid low for long enough and directed money his way, he'd leave me alone. But I heard from an old friend that he still wants me dead unless I satisfy him." He frowned. "Don't you see, Sonya? I'm taking a risk even being here right now. I want to be with you. I want to make up for the mistakes of the past, but I can't do that if I'm dead." He licked his lips and his eyes darted back and forth. "You said it yourself—a shadow blade. You live with the Dark Princess. Maybe if she put a good word in for me, Varga might back off. I have an opportunity coming up to help me accomplish exactly that."

Sonya stared at her father, her mouth agape. She sputtered something approaching a word before she finally managed to say, "You didn't contact me for all this time, and now you're here asking for favors?"

Clayton put his palms together. "I'm only saying it wouldn't hurt to ask. I think I can make it up to you if we spent more time together. I understand it might take months—even years—to earn your trust again, but don't you want to at least take the chance? Don't you want to be a family again? A real family."

"I…" She sighed and looked down. Every instinct in her, both innate and implanted by Tahir, told her that her father was full of crap, but not helping him was the same thing as sentencing him to his death. She couldn't help but feel that it wouldn't make her any better than him. Maybe she would kick him into the bay later, but for now, he at least deserved a chance. "Fine. I'll ask, but I can't guarantee anything."

Alison stared at Clayton from her seat at the conference table, her hands folded in front of her. This time, the full team had gathered. Ava took notes on her tablet and Hana, Tahir, and Mason sat scattered around the table. The fox glared at the man with open contempt, her eyes vulpine and her claws out, an open attempt to intimidate him. He glanced constantly at her, which suggested her tactic was working.

"Sonya asked," Alison explained. "So I'll give you your opportunity to speak, but keep in mind we don't trust you at all."

"Sure," he replied and swallowed awkwardly. His nervous gaze shifted to each team member every few seconds. "You have no reason to trust me. I'll make it simple. I did infomancy work for Varga—covering his trail during shipping, mostly. I got a little attack of conscience, and I had to run. I basically left him in a lurch, and he didn't take it kindly. I decided to come back recently because I came into money and I knew he would be in town. I thought throwing money at him might end this." He shrugged. "Varga's agreed to have one of his people meet me, but I could use people around in case he tries to kill me instead of talk."

Tahir shook his head, the disdain on his face more muted than his girlfriend's but still unmistakable. "There's an obvious solution. Why not go to the police?"

Hana snorted and nodded.

Clayton sighed. "I have one chance to get back with my girl. If I go to the police, there's no way I'll walk out of this without prison time. Worse, if I end up in prison—especially if anyone finds out I ratted on Varga—I won't walk out unless I'm a zombie. I'll admit, I've screwed up a lot, but I think I deserve a chance to survive and make it up to Sonya."

Alison nodded. "Here's what I'd suggest. We put in an appearance tomorrow at your meeting, merely to make sure it goes down without too much violence, and then we have another discussion about your future with your daughter."

His face brightened with hope. "Thank you. You don't know what this means." He pulled his phone out with a trembling hand. "Let me send the information on when and where we're supposed to meet."

Once Clayton left the room a few minutes later, Alison exhaled a long sigh.

"You don't actually believe any of that, do you?" Hana asked and shook her head in disgust. "It's all totally self-serving. You should have used a truth spell."

"I don't need a truth spell to know he's lying, at least partially." She shrugged.

Drysi snickered. "Then why did you agree to help the bastard?"

"Because as much as he wants to use us, I want to use him. The more of a Brownstone Effect we can establish in Seattle, the less trouble the other groups will be. We have a lot of the locals cowed, but people like Varga who aren't here full-time are a different story. I don't want to dismantle this guy's entire network, but I do want him to understand he doesn't get to kill people with impunity.

More to the point, maybe by protecting Clayton, other people who work for him might consider defecting. Besides, in the end, I don't think Sonya's eager for her dad to be killed."

"Not unless she does it herself," the fox muttered.

Drysi chuckled and Tahir shook his head.

"We'll go to the meeting tomorrow," their boss explained. "Either Varga backs off and this all ends, or we make him back off and this all ends."

"And after that?" Hana asked.

"Then it's like I said. We have another discussion with Clayton."

CHAPTER EIGHT

The Brownstone armored SUV rolled past the rusted gate of the abandoned factory, Mason at the wheel. Alison snorted as she studied their surroundings.

"You agreed to meet with Vargas's guys in a place like this?" she asked. "You might as well wear a sign saying, 'Please kill me.'"

The informancer shrugged from one of the back seats. "It's not like I'm in a position to argue with the man. He already wants me dead and I'm trying to change that. Why do you think I asked for your help?"

"I identify thermals of six men inside the building in front of you," Sonya reported through the comms. "The warehouse."

"I tagged three SUVs on a traffic camera miles back," Tahir commented. "They are all heading in your general direction, and very fast. All three are registered to one of the holding companies Clayton said Vargas controlled."

Hana smirked. "You're such a man of the people. They really, really want to make sure you don't get away."

"Right popular bastard, aren't you?" Drysi laughed.

He swallowed. "I'll square this with Vargas. He's a businessman. He has to see reason."

Mason stopped the SUV a dozen yards away from a black Lexus town car parked near the entrance to a crumbling warehouse. The loading bay was open, but darkness choked the inside where sunlight didn't reach.

"Defenses up," Alison ordered before she layered shields over herself. Mason cast his standard enhancement and shield spells, and Hana tapped her ring. She didn't fox out but she did retrieve her sword belt from the floor and strap it on. Clayton drew his wand in his trembling hand and cast a shield spell over himself. Drysi checked her daggers before she summoned her own shield and clucked her tongue.

"ETA of about ten minutes on the SUVs," Tahir reported.

"That gives us some time to chat. Nice." Alison opened the door. "I presume these guys are smart enough to use anti-magic bullets when dealing with a wizard. Be careful if they start shooting." She stepped out of the car and slammed the door shut. The others, including Clayton, filed out.

The doors to the Lexus opened. Four men in dark suits exited the vehicle and frowned. They advanced to within a few yards of the car and stopped to study the Brownstone team with suspicion.

Alison nodded to Clayton and moved forward. Her team moved with her.

Hana shoved Clayton toward the front. "Your fans await."

A man with a shaved head and a scar across his lips sneered at the infomancer. "Mr. Vargas didn't tell you to come alone, but I believe that was inferred." His voice carried a faint accent Alison couldn't place. He looked at her, obviously awaiting a response, but she nodded toward Clayton.

The other thugs kept their hands inside their jackets, ready to draw their guns.

"Long time, no see, Tamas." The infomancer chuckled nervously and shrugged. "Um…I merely thought I'd bring a few friends. I understand Mr. Vargas is mad at me, but I've tried to make it up to him. He got my message about the TrollCoin transfer, right? I only want to make sure that's enough to get us square again. It's a ton of money."

Tamas folded his thick arms across his chest and his suit strained with the action. "Business isn't always about money. That's something Mr. Vargas has long understood, but you don't. You were paid to do services for him but then decided you needed to leave him because you thought the authorities were too close. That's not okay."

Of course, Alison thought. *This is why I didn't need the truth spell.*

"T-that's not true," Clayton insisted. "I…couldn't handle it anymore. The work—I burned out. I gave the money back, or most of it. I had to take some of it to survive."

The other man sighed and shook his head. "You're so poor, huh?" He gestured to Alison. "So poor you can hire the Dark Princess as your bodyguard. I think you're insulting Mr. Vargas. Laughing at him. You think, 'Oh, I'm a wizard. He's a stupid piece of non-magical shit.' Is that what you think, magic man?"

She smirked. Maybe she shouldn't enjoy a thug threatening someone so much, but there were people who were due a little pain. Hana scoffed quietly, her hand resting on the hilt of her sword.

Clayton shook his head vigorously. "I don't think anything like that. I'm very grateful for the opportunities Mr. Vargas gave me, which is why I've spent this time earning way more than he ever paid me to show my respect."

"Respect?" Tamas spat at his feet. "You can't spell respect, maggot." His gaze flicked to Alison. "I'm surprised at you, Dark Princess."

"Oh?" she replied, raising an eyebrow. "Why is that?"

"I know your reputation. You are strong and brutal, but only against those you think deserve it. You're like your father and don't pick fights. Mr. Vargas has picked no fight with you, so why are you here? This wizard is scum. He's not worthy of your respect."

"I don't entirely disagree." She shrugged. "Then again, doesn't Mr. Vargas engage in trafficking? There are certain crimes I can't let go."

"Trafficking?" The thug scoffed. "Mr. Vargas is a religious man. Trafficking is slavery. He provides goods to people who want them. Maybe their government doesn't want them to have those goods, but who can trust the government? Everyone read about that Project Revenant. That's what the government does—it makes crude monsters out of good men. Mr. Vargas merely gives the people what they want. He doesn't violate their bodies and souls."

I don't know if I believe this man or not, but that doesn't

change the fact they've probably killed innumerable people—not
to mention whatever drugs and weapons they've brought in.

"I'm not a cop," Alison replied, "but this city is my
home, and I want to make it clear to certain people that
things are changing in Seattle. It's not business as usual.
Maybe you don't participate in human trafficking. Maybe
you're only arms and drug dealers." She paused and
glanced at him. "But there are many nasty drugs out there
—things like Ultimate."

Tamas's face twitched. "Ultimate." He swallowed. "We
don't even know what that is."

She laughed. "You guys are trying to bring it here, aren't
you?"

He managed an obviously forced grin. "Use a spell,
Dark Princess. I can honestly say we won't bring in any
Ultimate."

Clayton cleared his throat. "Um, aren't we getting off
track here?"

"Shut up, Clayton," both Alison and Tamas said at the
same time.

Hana snickered.

Alison let her arms hang loosely at her sides. If she
needed to cast a spell quickly, the stance would make it
easier. "Can you honestly say you didn't try to bring Ultimate in?"

"Ultimate's too hot. It's not worth the trouble." He
shrugged, a disappointed look on his face. "Even Mr.
Vargas says, 'Ultimate will bring the Granite Ghost.' Your
father does nothing for months, then he is in Vegas and
destroys the man supplying Ultimate. Maybe Mr. Vargas

could handle the Dark Princess or the Granite Ghost, but not both of you."

"Five minutes until reinforcements arrive," Tahir reported.

"The six in the warehouse have set up on either side of the loading bay door," Sonya added.

"So, maybe he screwed your boss, maybe he didn't." Alison gestured to Clayton. "I honestly don't care that much. I think his deal is fair. If Mr. Vargas is a business-man, it makes sense to take compensation and move on. Right now, he's not much on my radar, but that can change if I don't think he's a reasonable man. I don't need unrea-sonable men in Seattle."

"It's not for you to decide," Tamas growled.

The wizard waved a hand in front of him to get their attention. "Um, if Mr. Vargas has a bigger number in mind. I can get the money. I can get it into TrollCoin. Untraceable."

"There's no such thing anymore with magic." The mobster sighed. "Mr. Vargas has no desire to fight you, Dark Princess, but he can't let Clayton leave. It's bad for business."

She frowned. "Then we'll have a problem because he's coming back with me—alive. I don't volunteer to guard people only to hand them over to thugs to die, even if they are pieces of shit. That's bad for my business." She shook her head. "Tahir, do you think you can disable the SUVs?"

"Yes," he replied.

Tamas frowned and looked around. "Who is Tahir? Who are you talking to?"

"Do it then." She nodded toward her Brownstone SUV

and glared at her opponent. "Take his money already. Killing one piece of trash isn't worth getting on my bad side."

"It's nothing personal," he replied. "It's only business." He rattled something off in a language she didn't understand.

"Take them out without killing any of them," Alison ordered. She whipped her arm up and launched a stun bolt into the large man. He collapsed, his gun half-out and his eyes wide in surprise.

Poor asshole. He honestly thought that would work.

Mason cleared the distance in a few seconds and thrust his power-enhanced shoulder into one of the other thugs. His adversary managed to fire a single shot. The anti-magic bullet passed through the shield but only clipped the life wizard in the shoulder and he pivoted to pound another man in the chest. His target catapulted into the windshield of the Lexus. The glass didn't break and the man groaned rolled off the side of the car.

Reinforced?

The now foxed-out Hana pounced on the remaining man. She yanked the gun out of his hand and her claws dug deep into his muscle. He screamed and fell to his knees. She leapt up, her shielded knee out. It connected abruptly with the man's head, and he fell back as his eyes rolled.

The loud crack of a rifle sounded from the loading bay door. A bullet whistled past Alison's head. She layered another shield before she ducked behind the Lexus. She didn't want to test how well an anti-magic rifle round would do against her shields. The other Brownstone team members rushed to take position at the vehicle.

Clayton threw himself in front of the car, his hands on his head. "No, no, no, no. I'm going to die."

Hana patted his back. "You're a real brave guy, aren't you?"

Another few shots followed and the bullets bounced off the armored vehicle with a series of sparks. Brownstone Security wasn't the only organization to take safety seriously.

"Tahir, what's up with the reinforcements?" Alison asked.

"All disabled," he replied. "They're currently inspecting their vehicles, but I don't think they realize they've been EMPed."

"Sonya, position of the warehouse guys?"

"Three to the left, three to the right. They only spin out to fire."

She shook her head. "This should be easy then." She took a deep breath and pooled magical energy in her legs. "Everyone, give me cover fire if you can. I'll go on a count from five. Let's try to not kill anyone if we can."

Drysi and Mason nodded. The witch produced one of her glowing red explosive daggers, and he drew his gun.

"Five, four, three, two, one," Alison counted. She released the energy from her legs and launched herself toward the building.

The life wizard opened fire and alternated between the left and right sides but aimed high. Drysi arced a dagger as she stood a little too far away for a direct throw to reach the targets. The enchanted blade exploded in front of the door, and the two men who turned the corner to fire retreated, panic in their eyes.

Alison summoned shadow wings and continued toward the warehouse. She turned and threw several stun bolts toward her left side, which struck the distracted thugs without hindrance. The men didn't even manage a shot. When she spun to face the other three, she felled two with direct stun bolts to the head before they could fire. The last man managed a short volley before her attack eliminated him.

Her layered shields slowed the anti-magic bullets and deflected two. One ripped into her shoulder and she hissed in pain as it passed through.

"Damn," she muttered.

Mason jogged toward her as Drysi and Hana monitored the prisoners and Clayton. "Are you okay, A?"

She moved her shoulder and winced. "My shield took most of the punch out, but it's never fun to take a bullet." She drew a breath, raised her hand, and began the chant of a healing spell. "Ha. Maybe I should ask Rasila to tutor me on Drow shadow healing. That's another technique that requires more technique than raw power. It's like your parents said. I'm better at kicking ass than anything else." The flesh in her shoulder began to knit itself closed, and the pain ebbed.

Another thing Myna was beginning to help me with, too.

He shrugged. "In a couple of centuries, you'll be good at everything."

Alison sighed and rotated her healed arm a few times. "Let's collect our thugs."

The mobsters were all secured with the help of a conjured rope in front of the Lexus and on their knees. Alison smiled to herself, her arms folded.

Tamas glared at her.

"I want to make something very clear," she explained. "You're not dead because I'm all about giving people chances, despite the fact that you assholes tried to shoot us with anti-magic bullets. I take some small pleasure in realizing you merely wasted your boss' money and still had your asses kicked."

"That's really why you didn't kill us?" he asked.

"I'm also in a generous mood." She nodded toward Clayton. "And I'm trying to help him out for personal reasons. If I kill all Mr. Vargas's employees, that means he has more reason to want revenge. So here's how this will work. Clayton will transfer the money he promised, and you'll leave him alone. Right now, he's under the protection of Brownstone Security in the city of Seattle."

The wizard strutted in front of his adversaries, a huge smirk on his face. His confidence had soared once the Brownstone team finished their work. "That's right. If Vargas knows what's good for him, he'll back the fuck off."

"Shut up, Clayton," she yelled. She turned to Tamas and smiled. "I'm sure your reinforcements will be here soon, even if they have to take a Currus. They can untie you. I won't call the cops or anything. But please, explain to Mr. Vargas that whatever his beef is with Clayton, it's over. Seattle might not belong to me but it's my town and I do try to protect it. Understood?"

Tamas grunted. "Understood."

Alison pointed toward the Brownstone SUV. "Let's go."

CHAPTER NINE

Clayton marched around the Brownstone Security conference room, pumping his fist in the air. "Did you see the look on Tamas's face?" He laughed. "That bastard almost peed himself. That's what he gets for messing with Brownstone security."

Yeah, messing with Brownstone Security, Alison thought caustically.

She leaned against a wall, her arms folded. Hana sat beside Tahir and Sonya at the table. Mason and Drysi had volunteered to make a sushi run. It didn't feel like a full victory sushi day, but everyone deserved a treat after their help in an unusual family job.

Their visitor slapped a hand over his chest. "Vargas is probably crying right now. 'Oh, man, the Dark Princess is coming for me.'" He grinned. "He'll never dare touch me now. I wouldn't be surprised if he never lets his guys set foot in Seattle again in case you decide to go all Scourge of Harriken on him."

Alison cleared her throat. "How about the follow-up?

Now that we've taken care of the original problem, I think it's time for that."

He stopped and blinked at her in confusion. "Follow-up? What are you talking about?"

"Tamas made a few things clear to me before the fight." She lowered her arms. "And I'd like to use a truth spell to verify them. I don't think that's too much to ask given what we did for you."

The wizard frowned. "I'm not the problem here. Vargas is. Tamas was lying about the human trafficking. They do it. I swear they do."

"Then you wouldn't mind a truth spell, would you?" She smiled. "If you're not lying, you don't have anything to hide."

Sonya frowned at her father, disappointment in her face.

"Wait," Clayton replied. "What's going on?" He looked from Alison to his daughter. "We're good. Vargas won't touch me. We can be together again. Now, I have some business I need to take care of first—you know, tying up some loose ends—and I don't understand what any of this has to do with follow-up."

Hana rolled her eyes. "Maybe I should charm him. That might be a fun way to find out the truth."

"Charm me?" He frowned. "What is that?"

She gave him her best fox grin. "My own special magic."

"I don't get it. I'm the victim here. You were there. We tried to be reasonable and Vargas's thugs still tried to kill everyone. I was there to pay them off. I wanted this all to be over without any further trouble. I've done nothing wrong."

"Right. Pay them off." Alison snorted. "With whose money?"

"My money," he insisted. "Money I saved."

"You mean money you stole and stolen from whom, huh?" She walked over to the table, her eyes narrowed. "Here's my theory. I think you only came back because you heard about Sonya living with me. I think you thought you could leverage your relationship to get me to clean up your mess with Vargas. And you're right. I'm always willing to help out, especially in a family situation, but that doesn't mean I believed everything you told us."

"This is crap," Clayton sputtered. He looked at Sonya with pleading eyes. "You have to believe me. Everything I did was to make sure you were safe. I didn't ever intend to be gone this long. I know that hurts, Sonya, but I'll make it up to you as soon I have all those loose ends tied up."

Tahir leaned forward with a tight frown. "I'm willing to bet if I probed Vargas's activities that I wouldn't find any evidence of human trafficking. I'm sure I'd find all kinds of crimes, but probably not that one. I think you mentioned it because everyone knows how much Alison objects to trafficking."

"Even if that's true, it doesn't change the fact that he's a dangerous arms and drug dealer," the other man insisted. "And, uh…uh, I'm sure he's involved in trafficking. I'm not saying I can prove it in court or anything, but some of the records I saw? I kind of knew. I had a feeling. He's smart. It's not like he'll keep files listed as 'human trafficking records.' You have to look between the lines, you know?"

"That brings us back to the truth spell," Alison replied.

"It's a simple way to verify some of the things you've claimed."

Clayton threw his hands up. "Haven't I been victimized enough? Hasn't my daughter?" He pointed at Sonya. "We're finally back together, and you're ruining it with these wild accusations."

"Don't you have some loose ends to tie up first?" Hana asked, her voice sickeningly sweet but her eyes filled with malice.

"I can spend a few days with Sonya before taking care of that." He shrugged and smiled at the teen. "We have so much time to make up for."

Sonya scoffed. "I'm not a complete idiot, Dad. So stop acting like I am."

He staggered back. "What?"

"I wanted to believe that you came back for me and even held out hope after you asked about Alison protecting you, but let's be real. This has nothing to do with me except for me knowing the Dark Princess." She sighed and stared at the conference room table. "The more I think about my life, the more I wonder if you ever really cared. I bet you only needed a partner. Mom wasn't a magical, so she couldn't help you."

Her father shook his head. "It's not like that at all. I love you. You're my daughter. I'd love you even if you weren't a magical."

Alison sighed. "Yet again, we circle to the truth spell."

"Maybe there are some things I'm not proud of that I don't want getting out." Clayton shrugged and cast a nervous glance at her. "And it's not like you'll limit things. I appreciate your help, but that doesn't mean I'm ready to bare my soul to you, especially in front of my daughter."

"Bare your soul?" She shook her head. "You have no idea how true that used to be. How about this? What if I limit myself to one question? That's fair, isn't it?"

"One question?" He nodded slightly, pulled a chair out, and sat. "It depends on the question."

"I only want to ask you if the main reason you had for contacting Sonya was because she's connected to me. That's fair." She looked at Hana and Tahir and both nodded their agreement.

The wizard's face twitched. "No, that's not fair. You can have multiple reasons for doing something."

She nodded. "That's true. Then how about I ask you if your main reason for leaving Vargas was because the authorities were closing in rather than any moral concerns about your work?"

"Y-you're trying to make me look bad," he stammered. "But it's not like that. You can't reduce complicated situations to simple explanations. It's not how life works."

Sonya rolled her eyes. "That's so weak, Dad. I think, on some level, I always knew you were garbage and I always knew in my heart that you jetted because you cared more about yourself than me. But to see you here now, spewing such obvious crap? I can't believe you can do it with a straight face."

Clayton scoffed. "You believe Brownstone? She might have taken care of you for a while, but I took care of you for years. I'm your father. I'm the reason you even have magic."

"Screw you," the girl shouted. "Being nice to me every

once in a while doesn't make you a great father. I bet that Tamas guy is nicer to his kid if he has one. You have a responsibility beyond simply having me. I think about my entire life and it's not like I have many great memories of you. Admittedly, you were nicer when my magic came in, but I get it now. You saw a tool you could use."

He snorted and pointed at Alison. "Do you think the Dark Princess would care about you if you weren't a magical? You're only a tool to her, too." He waved his arm around. "She doesn't care about you. None of these people really care about you."

Hana glared at him. "Keep talking, asshole. No one has forced Sonya to help out."

Tahir nodded. "I provide training, but what she chooses to do with her future is her own choice. We are only in this position because of the substandard efforts of you and your wife. Your so-called parenting. To be frank, even if you only view your daughter as a resource for whatever criminal activities you're involved in, you've done a poor job of cultivating that resource. You're pathetic on several levels."

"Strangers," Clayton shouted. He banged his fist on the table. "You'll side with strangers over your own flesh and blood, Sonya? I'm your family."

Sonya shook her head. "No, you aren't. Not anymore. They're my family. They took me in when they didn't have to. They could have shoved me into the system and most people would say that was the right thing to do. It would have been easier for them, but I have friends now, and family. Adults who care about something other than if I'll be useful to them."

"Are you saying you choose them over your own father?"

Sonya took a deep breath and raised her head to stare at him, her gaze firm. "How about I choose the one question for the truth spell?"

"And what's that?"

"Did you even worry about me when you were gone?" Her eyes watered. "I don't care if you came back because of Alison or for any other reason. I only want to know if you worried when you were gone."

Clayton licked his lips. "You have to understand that I was on the run. I was distracted all the time. I didn't have time to think about a lot of things. Important things."

"Including your own daughter?" She slumped in her chair. "The only reason I'm not totally depressed is because I have Tahir, Hana, Alison, and all the others, but I never want to see you again. I was better off without you, and I understand that now."

"You ungrateful little bitch." He snarled his fury.

Hana stood as her tails appeared and her claws extended. "Give me a reason, asshole."

Alison shook her head. "He's not worth it."

The wizard scowled. "Whatever. Fine. I tried to be nice here, but if she wants to be a moody teenager, let her."

Tahir stared the man with a thin smile. "I don't think you paid close attention earlier when Alison talked to Vargas's man."

"Meaning what?"

"She made it very clear that her protection for you only extends to Seattle."

Clayton grimaced. "S-so what? I'll stay in Seattle. There's more than enough city here for me."

The infomancer shook his head. "Your presence here might prove distracting to my apprentice. I'll have to ask you on behalf of Brownstone Security to leave Seattle."

"What are you talking about?" He frowned. "Who are you supposed to be, King of Seattle?"

Tahir looked at his boss. "He's right. I might have over-stepped my bounds. Let me defer to actual royalty."

Alison shook her head. "I might not be Queen of Seattle, but I am the Dark Princess and Princess of the Shadow Forged, and I'll grant my royal permission to you this time, Mr. Arain."

He grinned. "Thank you. As I was saying, Clayton. Leave Seattle. We've saved your life but we don't want you around to upset Sonya. If you're smart, you'll keep a low profile lest Mr. Vargas becomes aware of you. We won't announce that we've asked you to leave, but if you force us to take greater measures, mistakes might be made."

"You can't do this," the other man shouted. "I came to you people for help."

"And we gave you help, despite you being unworthy of it. But we did that only for Sonya's sake." Tahir glared at him. "And now, you can help your daughter by leaving. You should be happy. This is one time where you being self-serving will actually help her out, too."

"Now get out," Hana snapped. "Before I decide to test my claws after all."

Clayton looked at Alison. She shook her head and pointed at the door.

"This is bullshit," he muttered as he stormed toward the

door. "You've taken everything out of context. I love my daughter. You're a bunch of self-righteous assholes."

"Would you be willing to submit to a truth spell about anything you've said?" she asked.

He paused at the door and glared at her. "Fuck you." Without so much as a glance at his daughter, he threw open the door and barged out of the conference room.

Sonya took a deep breath. "I'm sorry, everyone."

Tahir frowned. "Why are you sorry? You've done nothing wrong."

"I asked you to help him, but he turned out to be nothing but a dirtbag. I wasted your time."

The infomancer shook his head. "You needed your closure, and you have it. If he does care about you, maybe in the future, he'll reflect on his actions and truly try to make amends."

Hana smiled. "And even if he doesn't, you have us."

The girl wiped a few tears away and nodded. "Thank you. I don't know where I'd be without you."

The fox retracted her claws and released her tails. She headed over to the girl and pulled her into a hug. "Don't worry. We have your back. We're your new family, and we're a much cooler family than that loser anyway."

CHAPTER TEN

A few days later, Hana emerged from the shower in a robe, her hair in a towel and a smile on her face as she hummed a little off-key. Tahir sat at his desk and frowned at his computer. Omni slumbered peacefully on the couch in ferret form. It was a good night. It'd been a good few weeks, for that matter. She'd had a pleasant little Christmas break with Tahir and Sonya and felt good about the more recent successes.

We've kicked ass, and Sonya seems happier. It sucks that it's so cold and I can't wear my best outfits, but it's not like winter will last forever. I have my best pet and best guy. I'm loving this January. It's probably my best one ever.

"Curious," her boyfriend muttered. "And unexpected. Vexing, even."

"No one ever expects someone this hot, sure," she announced as she put her hands on her hips and thrust her chest out. Her robe didn't exactly flatter her figure, but he should get the point. "But I wouldn't call this sexiness vexing. You know what to do with it." She winked.

The infomancer didn't get the point. Instead, he responded with a grunt and didn't look at her. His attention remained fixed on the completely unsexy computer monitor in front of him, which was filled with text. She doubted it was erotic, too.

What could be so important to distract him from all of me?

"Are you paying attention to me, babe?" Hana asked. "Or are you in love with your computer now?"

"Obviously," Tahir replied. He flicked his finger on his mouse wheel to scroll through the messages on his screen and a frown appeared and rapidly deepened.

"Um, you're in love with the computer, or you're paying attention to me?" she asked, her voice wavering.

"I'm paying attention to you," he replied without looking at her.

Hana snorted. "If that's true, then what am I wearing?"

"I agree," he muttered. "Whatever you want. I think it's a good idea."

She rolled her eyes. "I'm totally naked and ready for you to take me on the kitchen table, babe."

"Yes, yes. Of course. A brilliant idea. I couldn't agree more. You should do that."

I hate when he does this. Does he honestly think it fools me? He might as well cast an illusion spell of him saying the phrases.

The fox marched over to his desk and snapped her fingers in front of him. "Hey, babe, pay attention. I'm talking to you. I don't mind if you're busy, but you can at least say, 'Hey, Hot Fox, give me a few minutes. I need to stop these hackers from launching an arsenal of nukes and starting World War III.'"

"World War III? Hackers?" He blinked in astonishment

and looked at her. "Sorry, I was distracted. You're right. It was rude to pretend otherwise."

"Yeah, I could tell you're distracted." She gestured to the screen. "What's the big deal? Did someone issue you a hacker challenge or something? And now you're preparing to defend your honor with a hack off? If it makes you feel better, I'm sure you have a hotter girlfriend than the hacker —or, if they have a boyfriend, I'm still hotter."

"No, if this was something like that, it would be far less surprising." Tahir nodded at the screen. "I received a message from someone inquiring about my previous posts looking for Omni's owner. They claim to be that person. It's pure luck that I even got these. I had those messages routed from different accounts, but I never stopped the forwarding filter. I meant to get around to it but I forgot once the mails died down."

"I thought you got rid of those posts super-deep, like infomancer scrubbed." Hana pushed at the air with her hands. "You know, whatever it was you did."

"Indeed, and that's why this is so curious." His frown became an almost-scowl. "It's as you've said. I was rather thorough. This is something that someone could have found on an Internet archive or something like that, and it's been some time since then." He tapped the screen. "In this case, the sender claims a friend of theirs mentioned it to them after a recent return to the area after being out of the country for some time."

I can smell a con, and this smells like an obvious one. I'm almost insulted by how weak the lie is. These assholes won't con me out of my magical pet.

The fox folded her arms. "Their friend remembered it

months later? This is a recent message, right? Not something that took forever to be forwarded?"

"Yes, the original message was sent about eleven hours ago, and such is the claim, but they are most insistent that Omni is their missing dog, who was then a puppy. They've even provided several pictures. I went ahead and analyzed them. They are high-probability matches. Almost perfect. Either they had previous pictures of him, or they've taken recent pictures of him and are using them, but I fail to see why they would go through the trouble unless they understand his true nature."

She glanced at the slumbering shapeshifting pet. "And they didn't say anything like, 'Oh, by the way, he might change shape?' That's his defining trait."

Tahir shook his head. "Not as such, no. Only that he's their dog, and they are eager to recover him. They've promised an unusually sizeable reward. It's not that impressive to people in our particular financial situation, but under other circumstances, it would be considered quite generous."

"But there's no way someone had him and didn't notice that he had his ability." Hana chewed her lip. "Or maybe he didn't develop the ability to shapeshift until later, or I unlocked it with my love."

"I'm dubious that you unlocked it with your love." Her boyfriend scoffed. "That's not a very likely scenario."

Ha. Sometimes you make it too easy.

She smirked. "And you're saying my love hasn't made you a better person? That's not what you told me before." She raised her eyebrows in question.

Let's see you wiggle out of this one.

The infomancer tilted his head and frowned in concentration for a moment, the barest hint of desperation in his eyes. "Yes, your love has made me a better person, but Omni isn't a person. We have no idea what he might be, but if this message is from his true owner, they might have some insight into his nature, and it might be worth meeting them for that reason alone."

The fox walked over to the couch and sat beside Omni. She stroked the sleeping animal's fur and exhaled a worried sigh. "And you don't think it's suspicious? He's their beloved pet which they lose and don't find until months later."

"Oh, it most certainly is, but sometimes, suspicious and difficult situations can still provide useful information."

She wrinkled her nose. "This sounds like an Alison 'we should step into the trap on purpose' plan."

"There is a certain wisdom in that strategy when you're out of options." He shrugged. "I'm only pointing out that we don't know much about him, and if this is from his true owners, we might be missing out on an opportunity to collect useful information about him—information we need to know."

"We don't need any special information. We've had him for a while now, and we've not had any trouble caring for him." She leaned over to nuzzle Omni. He stirred but didn't wake.

"And the mystery of his origins doesn't bother you at all? Not even a little?"

Hana shook her head. "I've told you before. I have no

interest in solving the mystery or whatever. Solving mysteries is overrated. I get that you're more intrigued, babe, but I don't really care about knowing everything. I only care about knowing enough, and I know enough to take care of him."

Tahir sighed quietly. "And you don't think his original owner has any right to him?"

"No." She frowned. "And I feel the same way about Omni's owner as I do about Clayton. Maybe I don't want to rip their balls off with my claws, but still."

He looked a little confused. "I don't follow your thought process here. Are you suggesting Omni's owner is some sort of criminal?"

"Not necessarily, but irresponsible fur-feather-scale parents are probably more likely to be criminals. I'm sure there's some study that proves it." She shrugged, impressed by her own impeccable logic. "My point is that they're irresponsible. I found him in the middle of a city, and they paid no attention or bothered to answer any of your initial ads. On top of that, they lost their beloved pet and then they left the country? They are horrible people who don't deserve a goldfish as a pet, let alone something special like Omni."

"Perhaps they had no choice." The infomancer shrugged. "There might have been important business considerations or something else of that nature. We can't assume too much about their character from Omni being on the streets. He might have turned into a form that allowed for an easier escape. We were only fortunate that he didn't escape when you first found him."

The fox shook her head. "There's no way he would ever leave me. My little baby loves his mommy." She beamed a smile at him. "Yes, he does."

He snorted and shook his head. "He might be a special animal, but he's still an animal in the end."

"And animals can still love their fox mommies," she insisted.

"Perhaps, but I think you've perhaps let emotion overwhelm logic here."

Okay, I need to lay this on the line and really make it clear to him. Either that or pull out the big guns, but I don't want to have to go that far.

She held a finger up. "I see two possibilities. One, they knew what he was and they were so irresponsible, they didn't take that into account, in which case, he shouldn't be with them." She held up another finger. "Or two, they didn't know, in which case they shouldn't have him because he's a special pet that requires special care, like the kind a wizard and a nine-tailed fox can provide."

Check and mate, babe!

Tahir folded his arms. "Do you claim, then, that in all cases when a pet owner loses a pet, they should cede ownership of it? That seems extreme and far beyond societal standards. In most cases, people seem eager to help reunite pets with their owners."

"I'm not necessarily saying that—at least not for all cases—but it's not like Omni's situation is normal, and this goes far beyond normal standards." Hana shrugged. "And if they took this long to respond for whatever reasons, I don't think they deserve him." She nodded. "And I don't

JUDITH BERENS

think you should reply. Omni's obviously happy with us. We can't break his little heart now. Or my little heart."

"This isn't like with Sonya. We can't know what he would prefer." He shrugged. "And we shouldn't simply make assumptions based on how you feel."

"Do you think he's unhappy? Huh?" She nodded at the still sleeping Omni. "Would an unhappy pet be so relaxed?"

"No, I'll admit he seems perfectly happy as far as shapeshifting pets go, but I'm simply pointing out that we can't be certain. Given his unusual nature, we might at least consider responding to the message."

"And how did responding to a message go for Sonya?"

"Again, the situations share some similarities, but they aren't the same," he replied.

Okay, time to up my game.

The fox stuck her bottom out. There was more than one way to charm a man. "And I'm asking you not to respond. I don't want to lose Omni, and I don't trust the message. I think sometimes not knowing isn't only better, it's also safer. We've run into that enough in the last year in the job and in our separate lives before that."

Tahir sighed. "Don't you think you're being a tad unreasonable in this situation? I know you care for Omni, but I think you're being too dismissive of the message."

"No, I don't think I'm being unreasonable. And I won't budge on this." Hana smiled at Omni. "I love my little all-purpose fur-feather-scale baby, and I won't give him up to some irresponsible loser who ran off to Malta or something after they lost him."

Her boyfriend shook his head. "The message didn't say anything about Malta."

98

"I don't care. My opinion is the same."

"Fine." He turned to his laptop. "I'll ignore the message for now, but I don't think it's the best course of action."

"Your opinion is duly noted and rejected."

CHAPTER ELEVEN

The man raised the camera to his face. Available magic in the world didn't mean that it should be used for every action and mission. Simple restraint meant less chance of detection on a planet still coming into its true power, and his organization's mission was too important to fail. The same could be said for automated technology. Drones were easy to disrupt or control, but it was harder to stop a man far away with a camera.

A beautiful dark-haired Asian woman walked down the street some distance away, the target on a leash in a canine form. Other people in his organization had already run the probability estimates. The match was unmistakable. The monster never changed size in its hidden forms to the best of their knowledge, one of its few weaknesses they had been able to exploit.

The man snapped a few pictures of the pair before he lowered his camera. He retrieved his phone and inserted a small black crystal into a port in the side before he dialed and raised it to his ear. He was a simple Strand, and he needed orders from his superior, a Weaver. All had their place in the Tapestry.

"Report," asked the Weaver.

"I have visual confirmation of the target. It's currently maintaining a canine appearance. An unknown woman is walking him."

"What species is the woman?"

"That information isn't available at this time, but she doesn't appear to be obviously Oriceran. I'll submit photos for facial recognition. The target is behaving within the parameters expected of its current form."

"It's fortunate we were able to constrain our search parameters with the collected intelligence. I was surprised to learn the target was so far from where we last saw it, but I suppose we shouldn't be surprised. Continue reconnaissance but do not engage the target or the woman. We need more intelligence if we want to stop it from escaping again."

The man raised his camera and snapped a few more pictures. "Orders received and noted."

Tahir finished typing and looked at the results of his analysis. Hana might have wanted him to leave the message alone, but every part of him cried out to solve the mystery. Ignoring it felt like he was admitting he wasn't good enough to discover the answer that underlay the mystery of Omni. As much as he loved her, he couldn't stand the idea of not at least checking into the message.

Despite all that, he accepted that she had a point and

was right to be suspicious. The timing of the message made him question its veracity and the people behind it. He doubted this was a simple case of someone having lost an unusual pet.

While he loved Hana's outlook, he didn't trust in her belief in the power of love to solve every problem, especially when it came to mysterious shapeshifting pets. Whoever was behind the message might have information, and the more he learned about them, the safer it would be to potentially approach them for a mutual exchange of information. This didn't have to end with Hana giving Omni up, but it also didn't have to end with ignorance on his part. He refused to let it end that way.

He frowned at his screen. His attempts to infiltrate the mail server where the message had originated using normal techniques had failed, which was both frustrating and unusual. He brought up a few spell scripts and executed them in an attempt to probe the server for magical defenses. Even though most companies still couldn't withstand even a basic's infomancer's efforts, such a situation wouldn't last forever, and it was never a good idea to assume it would. As magic and technology continued to fuse together on Earth to create something greater, basic security would grow to include magical security. Right now, only simple numbers protected many people's non-magical security.

I wonder how much people would panic if they realized that. The governments have been too slow or have handicapped themselves by being slow to integrate magicals into their many agencies. The world before the gates died when they started to open, and people need to accept that. If they do, perhaps they could be more prepared for the true future that is coming.

Tahir's frown deepened as he studied the new information that flowed across his screen. Why would some random pet owner need a magically hardened email account? Not only that but one that was able to stand up to one of his better spell scripts. Whoever had set the server up was no amateur when it came to magic, but they had made a critical mistake and revealed at least some of their charade. It wasn't much but it was enough that he was certain this wasn't merely a paranoid person paying a premium for more secure email.

The originating address of the message was listed as coming from a free commercial service based out of the Czech Republic. The infomancer was familiar with the service, as he'd hacked it several times in the past. He was also familiar with the feeble nature of its security, both conventional and magical. It was particularly notable because there was a Czech company that employed magic-hardened servers and was notoriously hard to hack, even for someone of his skills. It was very likely that whoever sent him the message hoped to conceal the magical defenses of their computers but didn't realize they'd made a mistake with their fake address. Or they'd merely hoped everyone would assume they used the other company and wouldn't notice the discrepancy.

He had encountered this kind of evidence numerous times. Hackers and infomancers sometimes focused their skills on specific areas and forgot the importance of the more fundamental knowledge- and social-based components of their work. A careful eye could identify something that even the most powerful algorithm spell might miss. Sometimes, a successful cyber-intrusion relied on the hacker knowing what to expect when he stepped inside a system.

It's definitely a fake account, and it was generated by someone with at least some access to magic. Now the question is, where do I go from here? I need more information, but what's the best way to go about gaining it without drawing too much attention to myself?

Tahir leaned back in his chair and scratched his chin. No one had ever accused him of being humble, particularly with regard to his computer abilities. In this case, however, he had no idea who the opponent might possibly be, and given that they were interested in Omni, it only raised the probability that they were something unusual.

Maybe Hana was right and it was best to leave the message alone for a while. It didn't mean he had to give up, but he could at least let the situation settle for a while which might put whoever he was facing off-guard.

In that case, it might be worthwhile to spend the rest of the night strengthening my wards and system defenses. Just in case.

He shook his head. Keeping secrets sometimes made sense, but it was time to be honest. He needed to talk to Hana, and they both needed to talk to Alison.

A shimmering three-dimensional image appeared in the center of the featureless circular white room. The image depicted the target in dog form being walked by the same woman the recon agent had identified.

"This is Hana Sugimoto," the Overseer announced to the other suited men who stood along the walls—his Weavers. Like many of them, he appeared to be nothing more than a brown-haired man in a dark suit with no distinguishing features and easy to lose in a crowd in many places. "She is a rare creature, a nine-tailed fox. Ironically, she's a shapeshifter. Perhaps destiny has guided the target to her." He spoke the sentences in a flat, almost monotone voice with no emotion on his face.

An image of Hana with her claws and glowing tails replaced the initial image.

"She can change into a normal-sized fox. When her tails are out, she has a form that we have determined is maximally efficient for tactical engagement. Her speed and agility are greatly increased. Please note, Sugimoto is also capable of a type of low-level hypnosis. All evidence suggests she's not an anomaly, but we don't have full confirmation of that fact at this time. She is quite experienced in psychological manipulation of people around her and has a history of such behavior."

Another image appeared, a white-haired, light-skinned woman holding a blade of pure shadow. Dark wings extended from her back. The image captured her in midflight over a large body of water, a determined look on her face.

"This is Alison Brownstone," the Overseer explained. "The so-called Dark Princess of Seattle. She is the adopted daughter of James Brownstone. He is also known as the Scourge of Harriken and the Granite Ghost, among other aliases."

One of the Weavers tilted his head in thought. "Previously, there's been evidence to suggest that James Brownstone is an anomaly. Do we no longer believe that is the case?"

"No, that information is still accurate at this time," he replied. "There is a high probability that he is an anomaly. It's too dangerous to target him directly based on all available evidence, and we've avoided close reconnaissance so as to not draw his attention. Currently, we have no agents capable of defeating him, to the best of our knowledge, even with full resources. He demonstrates unusual defensive resilience and possibly limitless regeneration abilities."

The assembled men all exchanged glances, their expressions flat and emotionless.

The one who had spoken nodded. "Doesn't that suggest Alison Brownstone is also an anomaly? Even if she is not in his genetic line, he might have subjected her to modification based on whatever hidden abilities are available to him. These considerations must be included in all estimates of potential actions against her or her subordinates such as this Hana Sugimoto."

The Overseer shook his head. "Our estimates suggest that Alison Brownstone's absolute power level exceeds many Drow of considerably greater age, but we do not believe she's an anomaly. However, there are some questions remaining about the New Veil incident in Washington DC, which she might have been involved in. Some evidence from that event suggests there is some small probability that she's an anomaly, but it's been difficult for us to gain information without alerting relevant agencies of the US government and their Oriceran allies. However, we do know her genetic samples are consistent with a simple human-Drow hybrid. We attribute her extreme power level to hybrid vigor at this time. There is also no evidence that Shay Brownstone-Carson, her adopted mother, is an anomaly." The images disappeared. "Alison Brownstone maintains a loose command structure over her subordinates, but each is unusually powerful or talented considering their background. This means any encounters with our Strands will involve extreme risk and likely necessitate the consumption of True Cores."

"We should isolate the subordinates of Alison Brownstone," suggested one of the other Weavers. "This will require separate teams of Strands."

He nodded. "Yes. There is a high probability that we will suffer heavy casualties, but it's necessary for the recovery of the target. There is a small chance that we will be able to persuade Hana Sugimoto to relinquish it, but available evidence suggests this is an unlikely scenario, and we should plan accordingly."

"If we can't risk drawing the attention of James Brownstone, can we risk drawing the attention of Alison Brownstone? If we eliminate any of her subordinates, that is a possibility."

The image of the nine-tailed fox walking the apparent dog reappeared.

"It's a risk. Our estimates suggest that in the vast majority of cases, James Brownstone does not involve himself in his adopted daughter's battles. A recent battle in Canada was unusual in that regard." He shook his head. "Indeed, all available evidence suggests an extremely low probability. We should be able to target Hana Sugimoto and recover the target without drawing unusual attention to the Tapestry."

He pointed toward the image. "In addition, we cannot allow the target to escape again. Heavy Strand casualties are acceptable and authorized. Isolate and engage whoever is necessary to recover the target. Use all available resources. Recovery is now of maximum importance."

CHAPTER TWELVE

"And that's my summary," Tahir finished. He sat at the conference table.

Alison rubbed her temples as she looked at Mason, Drysi, Tahir, Hana, and Ava. "You know this was supposed to be our slow time. Everyone was supposed to relax and train a little. Enjoy the winter and now, we've gone from dealing with guys firing anti-magic bullets to some unknown magicals interested in Omni. Next year, I'll simply have Ava schedule us constant jobs. At least we'll know what to expect."

Her assistant continued to type her notes. "I have turned down some well-paying jobs, Miss Brownstone. It'll be easy to do."

She chuckled. "I'll take that under advisement."

The way things are turning out, I wouldn't be surprised if Ava showed up in my office next week and asked us to help her rescue a long-lost daughter.

"The message might not mean anything all that important," Mason suggested with a shrug. "It might even be a mistake or a coincidence."

The infomancer shook his head. "Too many points of data suggest otherwise. Omni's unusual nature is a major red flag and combined with the fake account and the magical protection, that at least suggests people of decent means are interested in him and that could be trouble. The pictures sent matched too closely for this to be a case of simple mistaken identity. No, whoever sent that message is definitely interested in Omni and has some decent magical ability, including infomancy."

Hana scoffed. "Skulking around with fake accounts. Talk about bad fur-feather-scale parents. I don't have fake accounts."

"I do," he noted with a shrug.

"Well, I'm the mommy, and you're only the boyfriend."

Alison sighed. "I'm sure they probably are bad pet parents, but we have to face the truth that Omni is something unusual. If they're sniffing around, we need to look into this more. We literally don't know what we're dealing with. I've thought for a while, now, that something like this might come. I hoped it wouldn't come quite so soon, but it is what it is."

"Why do we have to look into it, though?" the fox complained. "If we ignore it, they'll go away."

"I doubt that," she replied.

"They'll confront us eventually if we don't," Mason replied with a shrug. "If they are already taking these kinds of measures to hide who they are, it screams some shady organization that lost something important. After what happened with Project Revenant, for all we know, Omni's some sort of government experiment—their chameleon spy dog or something."

Drysi nodded. "I'm not saying this involves dark wizards, but you all know how the Seventh Order devised plans over decades. Some bastards are bloody patient, especially magicals."

"I fully intend to spend additional time investigating," Tahir confirmed. "But I wanted to clear it with you first, Alison, in case I brought trouble down upon myself or the company. I can't say it's impossible. I don't know who we're dealing with."

"Go ahead and do your thing." Alison frowned. "We've let this slide for far too long. We should have discovered what Omni was and where he came from a long time ago. That's the only way to make sure we're all safe, including him. I know it's tough. These days, you never know if something's more dangerous than it appears. A simple artifact might be a doomsday device in the wrong hands, but Brownstone Security is supposed to make the city safer and I have to be aware of the dangers Omni might represent."

Hana muttered something under her breath. She glared at Tahir, and it was obvious he wouldn't get any for a while. To his credit, he returned his angry girlfriend's glare with a calm look.

Her boss glanced at her. "Hana, you also need to face the reality that depending on what Omni is, you might have to give him up for either your safety or the safety of others."

"No way, no how. And safety? What are you talking about?" Hana shook her head. "I don't care if he is a government project. He hasn't killed campers or even growled at anyone when we go on walks. He's way nicer than most of the other pets I see in my neighborhood. There's zero evidence that he's dangerous, and it's not like I'm home all day to watch him. If he wanted to sneak out and eat kids or something, he's had plenty of opportunities." She pointed at Tahir. "He even had those cameras on him for a while."

"Those only made it so he couldn't transform," Alison replied. "Maybe they limited his ability to also turn into anything dangerous."

"Maybe, but it wasn't like he walked around and got on the computer and ordered a thousand pounds of Indian food as a prank when I wasn't there." She sighed. "I won't give him up because someone is looking for him. That's not good enough. Not after all this time. Just because he transforms doesn't mean he's dangerous. It only means he's cool."

"I understand that, and I understand where you're coming from." Her boss shrugged. "I'm only saying you should at least prepare yourself for the possibility. You need to be mature about this, Hana. This isn't me saying you need to take care of Old Yeller yourself, only that he might need to be handled by someone with the appropriate training."

"Old Yeller?" The fox's expression turned quizzical. "And I handle him fine."

"It's a...never mind. It's not important. but prepare, okay? Or at least think about preparing for the possibility." Alison drew a deep breath.

I'm half-convinced Omni has some kind of fox-like charm

ability the way Hana fawns over him, but it's not like she doesn't have a weakness for cute things.

Hana harrumphed. "I'll prepare for the *small* possibility, but I won't agree to anything without decent information and not some suspicious liars who are looking for Omni." She shook a fist. "And I'll only give him up if, like, it's necessary to save the world or if I have reason to believe his original owners—who couldn't even keep him from getting lost—aren't total suspicious assholes. So far, they haven't done much to convince me of that. I'm damned lucky to have such a special pet, and short of going to Oriceran, I don't think I'll find another one that cool ever."

"Need to save the world?" Drysi snickered. "What if you only need to give him up to save a city? What would you do then?"

"I don't know. It depends on the city." She shrugged. "We could do with fewer cities."

The Welsh witch laughed.

The sad part is I'm not sure if she's joking or not, but we need to get this situation under control one way or another.

Alison frowned in thought. "I wonder if we should reach out to someone."

Tahir frowned. "Such as who?"

"I don't know. The PDA, maybe? Fish and Wildlife? NOAA?" She shrugged.

"If the PDA were tracking this animal, they would probably have already asked for your assistance," he observed. "Or they would have responded to my ads when I first posted them. I find it hard to believe they wouldn't have actively searched for something like that."

She looked at Ava. "And no one's reached out recently. Maybe you merely wanted to give me a little break?"

The woman shook her head. "No one from the PDA has passed any information to us or made any requests that might suggest they are looking for a creature similar to Miss Sugimoto's pet," she responded. "And I can assure you, I would never filter PDA information even if I thought you were overworked, Miss Brownstone."

"Okay, fair enough. Just checking."

"And as has been pointed out, efforts such as Project Revenant suggest we might not want to attract the government's attention if possible," Tahir suggested. "While I trust Agent Latherby, we can't be certain that every government agency or agent is as dedicated to the welfare of citizens. Hana might be right. Omni might not be dangerous, but that might only be because he's not been modified by some government program."

Alison sighed and nodded. "I worry that we're sitting on a time bomb. After that crap with Raven, I was reminded of how even a few magicals can cause trouble if they get their hands on the right crap."

"Omni's a time bomb?" Hana rolled her eyes. "Why? Because someone wants him? How has he gone so long without hurting someone if he's so dangerous? It's hard for me to think of him as deadly when he's not only adorable, but he's also never actually done anything mean or threatening."

"Maybe no one's given him a reason to hurt anyone," Drysi commented with a shrug. "That doesn't mean he won't be a right angry bastard and ready to kill if someone does. I've known many people with sweet dogs who would tear your throat out if you threatened their owner."

"Yeah, kind of like my dad," Alison agreed.

"The reality is that we have to deal with the implications of the message," Mason commented. "At the minimum, it means someone knows Omni's in the Seattle area. We already know he's hard to track, but that at least narrows the area down if they weren't sure."

"How easy can it be to find a little brown animal who can change shape?" Hana asked with a shrug. "I only take him for a walk in dog form most of the time, and he's tiny."

"It depends on how lucky they are," he replied. "If they knew what they were looking for, they could also hack cameras or drones to help accelerate the process."

Tahir nodded. "There was little identifying information in my original posts asking about him. There was nothing to help demarcate particular portions of the city, so even if whoever sent the response has the original messages, they don't have anything more specific than Seattle proper. Even if they exclude certain neighborhoods due to baseline socioeconomic filters, that leaves considerable ground to cover."

"We've been able to track people and we're not a huge company, which means they might be able to achieve something similar." Alison took a deep breath. "I think I'll have to go a little with Hana's gut on this."

The fox's expression brightened, and she clasped her hands together. "Really? I mean...that's right, listen to Hot Fox. I know what's up. Time for the Pro-Omni Party to rise."

"Really?" Tahir echoed and doubt filled his voice. He

offered his girlfriend an apologetic look. "It's not that I don't enjoy Omni, but I think some valid concerns have been raised."

"I'm not saying I agree with all of Hana's arguments, but I'm not about to trust somebody who has already lied to us via the account they're using," she explained. "I want us to be able to approach these people with more information so we have some kind of context to begin negotiations. I don't think that's crazy or irresponsible." She looked around.

Mason nodded, along with the infomancer. Drysi shrugged. She looked more amused than worried. Delight had suffused Hana's face.

"You haven't responded at all to the message in any way?" Alison asked.

Tahir shook his head. "No, I haven't. I wanted to get everyone's input before I committed us all to a potentially dangerous course of action."

"Then I suggest you should respond with a lie." She shrugged. "Tell them you already gave Omni away. That will at least put them off our scent and give us time to find more information."

Drysi ran her tongue inside her cheek. "Tell them you gave him to a wizard collector from out of the country. I don't know. Cyprus or something."

Mason laughed. "Cyprus?"

"What do you want me to say? Bloody Wales?" She snorted. "The point is somewhere unusual and where it'll be harder for them to investigate. I know a thing or two about laying down a false trail. These days with magic and things like the trains, people can't dismiss unusual country connections for magicals."

Their boss nodded. "Whatever. Or pick Oregon. But make it seem like you don't have Omni anymore. If they want contact information for the person you allegedly passed him on to, say you don't have any. It's not like you've claimed to be a breeder. There's no reason for you to carefully track who a stray dog went to, and if they ask anything strange or hint about his abilities, we'll have at least gained more information."

Tahir nodded. "And if they press the issue without revealing more information?"

"I trust in your and Hana's ability to make up a convincing lie." She shrugged. "They don't know anything right now other than you put up some ads for a lost puppy months ago and then pulled them down."

Ava cleared her throat. "And you're sure that you don't think the creature is a danger?"

Alison shook her head. "I'm not sure about that at all, but right now, he has months of being a good boy as evidence in his favor."

The fox smiled. "Exactly. He's a good boy. He's all the good boys in one."

"And if he turns out to be a bad boy?"

"Girls love bad boys," she countered.

The infomancer snorted. "Does that make me a bad boy?"

She winked. "Yes."

CHAPTER THIRTEEN

Several days later, Alison and Mason strolled along the street after a pleasant meal at a French restaurant. It'd been warmer the last few days, which mostly meant the snow had melted off and there were no additional falls forecast for a few weeks. It might have been the end of the white winter for Seattle, but that only made it chilly and wet.

Alison felt no guilt for her date night, despite the concerns over the suspicious communication. Until they had more information, the team had nothing to act on. Tahir continued his attempts to probe and to track the sender but to his frustration, had reached a dead-end. Whoever they were, they hadn't responded to his message to say they'd given Omni to a dog collector who claimed he was a rare breed. They'd settled on a Welsh collector in the end.

I wonder if dark wizards are now running all over Wales looking for Omni, or maybe mobsters or Nerak poachers. The line separating Earth from Oriceran is blurry already, and the gates are barely open. Earth won't look like Earth in a few hundred years.

There's always trouble happening, but life goes on. We have to keep living. There's no other choice, really. If I stopped and always waited for the hammer to fall, I would never get anything done. And if I really do live a long time, I need to appreciate every moment I have.

She laughed at a sudden realization.

Mason looked at her in query. "What's so funny, A? I thought you just said how much you liked the restaurant and appreciated all the flavors there. It had good reviews, and my food tasted good." He shrugged.

"Oh, I loved the restaurant." She shook her head. "What I was laughing at had nothing to do with that."

"What then?"

"I think you and Hana have changed me," she explained. "And some of the others, too, of course, but mostly you and Hana."

"Changed you? I hope it was in a good way." He grinned. "I don't see how you're different, though. You're still the same woman I fell in love with."

"That's sweet, but I have changed. I thought about how I still wanted to have my date night despite all this crap." She shrugged. "The old Alison—even the woman you met when we first started dating—wouldn't have thought about that. She would have been too concerned about taking care of everything and anything before she dared to have any fun. It's one of the reasons I had no life, basically, before I moved to Seattle. It was the job all the time, and if it wasn't the job, it was dark wizards or training. I felt more guilty about taking any time away from that."

She smiled. "Hana helped to start breaking me out of thinking like that and you finished the process. It's only funny to realize how far I've come in such a short time. We were talking with your parents about how long I might live, but I've changed so much already and I'm still young, even for a human."

"There's nothing wrong with a little relaxation or healthy change." Mason put her arm around her and pulled her close. There weren't many other people on the cold street, but numerous cars passed them.

"I've always known that but it's taken me a while to truly accept it," she replied. "I don't know. I suppose I felt, on some level, like I didn't deserve to have a normal life while bad things were happening, especially because of what happened to my mom—my biological mom, I mean." She frowned. "I hate referring to her that way. I loved her as much as I love Shay, but..." She shook her head. "That was the beginning of everything for me. It's not like I had a totally carefree childhood before that, but it was a lot to take in as a teen, especially since my father was the one who betrayed her to the Harriken."

"Don't overthink it. Stay as the new Alison." His expression turned thoughtful. "The thing is, we both know there are always bad things happening. If not in your city, then in your state, if not in your state, then in the country and if not in your country, then another country. But it's not any one person's responsibility to stop all those bad things. That's the point of having society. Even your dad knows that."

Alison shook her head. "But he's not like me. It's not that he doesn't care, but he's always been far more about,

'Leave me alone, and I won't punch you.' You could argue that I go looking for more trouble. He didn't set out to establish a Brownstone Effect. It simply worked out that way, but I've tried to achieve it deliberately. I started a security company because it was the most efficient way I could think of to leverage my bounty-hunting skills into protecting people."

Mason smiled. "Then don't worry about any of it and simply enjoy date night. Let this new relaxed Alison live. I'm sure we'll find out that the government created ten Omnis to destroy the planet or something annoying like that, but until we do, there's no reason not to enjoy our time together. We can't know what tomorrow will bring. All we can do is enjoy the present."

She stopped abruptly and turned her head toward a brightly lit shop beside her. Dozens of necklaces and expensive rings stood on stands in the window display.

"What is it?" He followed her gaze. "Did you see something?"

"It's a jewelry store," she explained as a silly idea percolated in the back of her mind.

"I can see that." He shrugged. "There are a few of them in this neighborhood."

Alison smirked. "Maybe we should go in there and look at some rings since we've talked about that kind of thing. It might be good to get an idea of what's available."

He nodded, a serious look on his face. "Yes, maybe we should. That's not a half-bad idea."

Damn it.

Her heart rate kicked up. It'd been a joke and she'd not expected him to call her bluff.

Mason leaned toward her ear and his hot breath tickled the sensitive skin there. "I have something to tell you," he whispered. "Something important. Something you need to hear right now."

Oh, crap. I told him not to make it epic, but now's not the greatest time. Then again— Whoa. Wait. Am I ready for that already?

"What is it?" Alison asked, shivering but not from the cold.

"We're being followed," he whispered. "I think we should go into the store to see if whoever it is gives up. There aren't many people on the street, but between the stores and cars, if we start anything, it'll get messy."

"I'd love to check out rings, sweetie," Alison replied, her voice at normal volume. There was no reason to let him know he'd won the bluff war. She forced a huge fake smile on her face. "I want the best ring for the special day."

He snickered and winked. "I'm sure you do, and I want to make sure you get it."

I don't know if I should be freaked out that he seems so happy about fake ring shopping or annoyed that some assholes are trying to mess up my date night. I wonder who it is. At this point, there's a rich list of suspects to choose from.

Mason opened the door and gestured inside. She entered and enjoyed the rush of warmth over her chilled face. Diamonds, gold, and silver glittered under the bright lights of the store.

A young raven-haired saleswoman with the perfect chignon and an even more perfect diamond hairpin through it clasped her hands together and rushed toward them. "You probably get this all the time, but has anyone told you that you look exactly like Alison Brownstone?" Her smile widened. "The resemblance is uncanny. It's not like I've met her, but I've seen her on the news."

She shrugged. "Guilty as charged, but that makes sense because I actually am Alison Brownstone."

The woman's eyes widened, and her mouth formed a perfect "O." "I'm so honored that you would choose to shop here." She gasped. "You're not the first celebrity to come here. Did someone recommend you? I heard you're friends with Jericho Cartwright. Did he recommend us to you? He bought a necklace here for a girlfriend when he was in town filming—a beautiful piece. I was so jealous." The diamond necklace she wore could probably feed a family or two for a long while.

Alison shook her head. "Uh, I've been near him, but I wouldn't exactly say we're friends."

Mason threw his arm around her shoulder again. "I'm glad you're so enthusiastic. We're here to look at engagement and wedding rings."

Oh, come on. We didn't need to play it up inside too.

"Oh, my," the saleswoman squealed. "The problem with you, Alison, is there's so little in the news about your personal life, only all those criminals you deal with." She studied Mason. "I'd heard you were dating someone from your company, but I didn't know he'd be so handsome." She grabbed Alison's free hand and tugged her toward a display case. "I have some great suggestions. Perfect for someone as special as you."

Well, great. Now every gossip site in the country will talk about my upcoming wedding that's not even happening. Not anytime soon anyway. Damn it. I need to focus. There's someone following us, and Mason is taking the opportunity to mess with my head.

She glanced out the front window. An elderly couple wandered past. They could be disguised assassins, but they didn't look at her and she didn't sense any magic from them.

When she turned again, the saleswoman pointed to a ring with a huge yellow stone that looked like it should be used in siege engines to destroy walls rather than worn on anyone's hand.

"Now, I understand that as a part-Oriceran, you need a special ring," the assistant suggested. "We don't have anything magical at our particular shop, but it's not like anyone expects their engagement and wedding rings to have actual powers, right? Merely the power of beauty and elegance?"

Well, Mom's rings do, but that's unfair. And I haven't...I'm really getting sucked into his.

The woman tugged her forward and pointed at another ring. The latest piece was filled with so many facets it might as well have been its own mine. "I suppose I should have asked this in the beginning." She glanced from Alison to a grinning Mason. "What price point are we looking at? It never helps to assume."

"Oh, price isn't a concern," he replied. "You can't give an engagement ring to a princess if you quibble about price." He winked.

Very funny, Mason.

The saleswoman nodded, her face deadly serious. "I so agree." She turned to Alison. "If you want, I can give you my card, and I can do some research on Oriceran and

Drow rings, Miss Brownstone. Or...do you prefer Princess Brownstone?"

Alison grimaced. "Alison's fine, and even if we did use my title, I'm not Princess Brownstone. I'm Alison, Princess of the Shadow Forged, but only..." She sighed. "Let's look at more rings."

Thirty minutes later, they stepped outside with the woman's card in both their pockets and having experienced a fine and thorough tour of the most expensive rings in the store. Alison had learned more about how to evaluate rings in that short trip than she had in her entire life.

"That was fun," Mason quipped with a smile, and his gaze swept their surroundings. "Unfortunately, it didn't solve our problem." He slipped his arm through hers and continued up the street. "Our friends are still there," he whispered. "It's like they waited for us the entire time. Several men—brown-hair, dark suits. No obvious wand holsters, but they might have them concealed. Or they might be non-magicals with a few surprises of their own."

She frowned but didn't bother to look over her shoulder. It would be too obvious.

"We're still not in a good position to fight," she whispered in response. "Even if I use my wings and attack them, they'll still manage to fire and might hit someone."

"The parking garage," he suggested. "There will be fewer people there, and it's more contained. It'll help stop rogue bullets or spells. Maybe we can even head in there and hide with a spell until they get bored and leave or confront us."

"The parking garage?" She groaned. "What about my Fiat?"

"Priorities, A." He winked. "Unless you have a better plan?"

"I don't, but if my car is blown up, I'll make you explain it to Mom."

CHAPTER FOURTEEN

"Nothing like a little night walk," Hana sang. She held lightly onto a leash connected to Omni, who currently was in his original—and, in her opinion, most adorable—form as a small dog. Even though she didn't need the leash, she didn't want to deal with the inevitable disapproval she'd receive if she walked her dog without one.

They strolled down the sidewalk in a park near her home. The lights strung high on poles pushed the shadows away—not that she was worried. Anyone who attacked them would experience the fun of fox claws, and it was a nice neighborhood anyway. When she saw police, it was almost always them pulling someone over for speeding.

That's the way it works, huh? If you have money, you can move away from all the crime, and if you don't, you spend your time worrying about crime. I never worried much because of my charm and claws, but what if I was merely a normal orphan girl who ended up on the streets?

She shook her head, not sure why she worried about

that kind of thing. Thinking about what might have been was pointless. She did have powers, money, and the best pet in the world. While she doubted she even needed to walk him, she felt bad that he was stuck in the house or yard all the time. Every creature craved something greater, and a nighttime stroll was the easiest way to give him a taste of the world.

"I can't believe everyone thinks my baby is dangerous," Hana complained to Omni. "The funny thing is, of the two of us, I'm the dangerous one. I've seen chihuahuas scarier than you, and I'll not give you up because of people's paranoia. That's silly. I think Tahir's annoyed that he can't infomancer his way out of a problem, and he's blown this up into something more than it is."

Omni looked over his shoulder at her, his head tilted slightly before he turned forward again.

Hana snickered. "Yes, you're the deadly time bomb I'm supposed to worry about. Maybe we should take you to that disposal witch so she can send you to whatever weird dimension she's polluting." She inhaled deeply and wrinkled her nose. An odd scent filled her nostrils, weak but noticeable. A hint of magic with something else she couldn't identify.

The fox and hound continued down the pathway of the empty park. Unsurprisingly, most people weren't in love with the idea of walking around a muddy park when the temperature was in the thirties, let alone during a cloudy night. The confluence of disagreeable circumstances culminated in Hana blinking in surprise when a brown-haired man in a dark suit stepped onto the path in front of her. She didn't recognize him, but something about him was so generic that she thought she might have trouble remembering him even if she met him again.

Some guys simply aren't lucky. Even if he were ugly, it would at least give his face some character rather than him being Captain Generic.

She slowed as he strode toward her. He neither smiled nor frowned but simply stared at her, his face blank and almost lifeless. There was no anger in his eyes or lust, merely the barest hint of interest.

"Can I help you?" she asked.

The stranger stopped a couple of yards away and his gaze dipped to Omni. "Breed?"

"Excuse me?" Hana asked with a frown. She prepared to fox out and teach the freak a few things.

"Your dog's breed," he clarified. His voice was flat and monotone as if they were having the most boring conversation in the world. "I want to know it. Please tell me if it's not too much trouble. I don't believe that it should be."

She chuckled, relieved that she wouldn't have to rip someone's throat out during her walk. "And here I was saying, 'Whoa, pal, we just met.'" She shrugged and nodded at Omni. "I actually don't know his breed. To be honest, he's a little of everything, I think. I'm not an expert, but that's the feeling I get."

"I see. That's very interesting, and I don't mean to be presumptuous, but did you find your dog as a stray or was he from a shelter?"

A cold shiver ran through her body at the man's inflectionless voice. It was like talking to a robot in a suit. She inhaled deeply. The strange scent from before was stronger.

What the hell is that? Some weird artifact he has on him? He doesn't look tense or like he's about to attack me, but he's definitely not acting normal either.

"He's a stray, actually," Hana explained. "I found him one day and I knew what I had to do. Who could leave this adorable little guy on the mean streets of Seattle?" She crouched and scratched Omni behind the ears. "I love my little fur baby, even if I found him on the street."

The man nodded. "That's interesting. Extremely interesting. Unexpected, perhaps."

"Interesting?" The fox stood and lowered her arm, only a few fingers now on the leash. She didn't know how Omni would react if she attacked someone. When she'd foxed out in front of him before as a test, he hadn't seemed frightened or more interested in her than normal. "What's so interesting about that? Many people adopt strays. More people need to adopt strays."

"I don't doubt that truth," the man replied. "That's not what I find interesting. Your behavior is irrelevant in this regard."

She frowned. "Okay, then what are you saying?"

"I have a friend," he explained. He pointed at Omni. "This friend, John, is missing a dog very similar to yours. He told me it is a mixed breed. I'd like to take a picture of yours and show it to him. I'd also like some contact information for you in case it is his dog. I'm sure you can understand that he would like his pet back for the same reasons you enjoy its company."

Hana's fingers twitched. If the man had even the slightest hint of emotion in his face, she might have thought he was hitting on her and tried to trick her into giving him her phone number. The inflectionless monotone that defined his speech made everything he said seem as if he was bored and vaguely sinister. Which still left her with a creepy man chatting her up in the middle of a park by herself.

It's not like every serial killer is charming, right? He pops up out of nowhere in the middle of the park to talk to me alone and sounds like he has no emotions. If that's not serial killer material, I don't know what is.

Hana frowned. She wasn't worried about getting in trouble if she defended herself, but the strange scent worried her. The man was more than he appeared, and that meant there was a risk not only to herself but Omni as well. If she could avoid a conflict, it would be best, but she had no way of knowing what was going on in the man's head.

Maybe I should try charming him, but I have a feeling that would take too long.

"I'm sorry for your friend," she replied. "But I'd rather not let strangers take pictures of my dog. We advertised when we found Omni. No one came forward, and so he's my dog now. I won't give him up to someone who was so irresponsible that he was found wandering the streets."

"Omni?" The man tilted his head and blinked. "An interesting choice of a name."

"I liked the sound of it." She tugged at the leash and turned to leave. "And I have to head back home now. My boyfriend's expecting me, so if you'll excuse me. It was interesting talking to you."

"I understand your reluctance to part with Omni. Pets are like our children." He nodded but once again, no expression mirrored the sentiment on his face. "Go now and enjoy the company of your pet. I will trouble you no longer. Thank you for your conversation."

I swear this guy has blinked only a couple of times this entire conversation. Is he on something?

"Thanks for that," she responded and allowed suspicion and disdain to color her face. She hurried away with Omni in tow and glanced occasionally over her shoulder. The stranger stood and stared at her, his hands at his sides.

The fox exhaled a sigh of relief when the path curved away and she was no longer in his direct line of sight, but tension suffused her body a moment later. She looked around slowly. No one was there, but it didn't feel like it.

That creep must have followed me. Someone's watching me. I can feel it.

She sniffed the air. The strange scent from before was everywhere, now, and much stronger. Some of it resembled magical scents that seemed familiar to her, but she had no basis of comparison for the other aspects of it. It was rare that she ran into something that didn't smell like anything she'd ever encountered before. Even during her trip to Japan, most of the magical scents remained cloaked in familiar smells. She didn't know whether to be excited or frightened.

I shouldn't be scared. I don't care who or what creeper boy is. I'm a nine-tailed fox and I work for Brownstone Security.

I shouldn't be frightened of anyone in this park. They should be frightened of me.

"What the hell is that smell, though?" Hana muttered. She stopped and frowned. "Okay, Omni, I'm sure I'm being followed, and so the question now, boy, is do I stay here and kick their asses, or do I go back somewhere with actual people? That might discourage someone from trying something, but if they do, it means there's more risk to other people. On the other hand, I am Hot Fox, Alison Brownstone's right hand. Even without my defensive artifacts or my sword, I kick ass, and if this is only about some creeper in the bushes, he'll find out why hunting around here is a terrible idea. Maybe for true safety, you do have to make a few examples every now and again. Call it the Sugimoto Effect."

The emotionless man from before stepped onto the path in front of her.

"Hey, asshole, this isn't funny," she protested.

"I never said it was," the stranger replied and regarded her steadily.

It took her a few seconds to realize it wasn't the same man, merely one who dressed, sounded, and looked similar. Several others stepped from behind bushes and the scent built with each one.

Okay, now this isn't fun. I didn't expect his buddies.

"I think I left my oven on," Hana said. "Sorry." She turned smartly and led Omni down the path leading out of the park. She had barely covered twenty yards before several more men stepped out of the bushes to hem her in. The plain-looking men in suits now surrounded her on all sides, their expressions uniformly blank.

Omni looked at them and his hackles rose. He uttered an uncharacteristic growl.

She snorted. "Yeah, if you want to be dangerous now, I don't mind."

CHAPTER FIFTEEN

One of her harassers stepped forward. "I would ask you to surrender the animal." He looked no different from the others and sounded very much like the man she had talked to earlier.

"And why should I do that?" Hana challenged. "Give me one possible reason why I would give my dog to the weirdest gang in Seattle? Is this your thing? Going around town at night stealing people's dogs? Because I don't really like you right now, and to say I'm as suspicious as hell is the world's biggest understatement. Haven't you guys heard of James Brownstone? What he did to the Harriken? Doesn't that make you think twice about trying to take someone's dog?"

These guys might have nothing to do with the message. It might simply be a coincidence.

"No, not dogs. That would be pointless." The man shook his head and pointed at Omni. "You have been observed, Hana Sugimoto. Our estimates suggest a high probability that you are aware that the animal you call

Omni is no dog. The mere fact that you refer to it with that name increases the possibility of that truth. You don't need to be harmed. We only ask you to surrender the creature. After that, you are free to leave and you will never see us again. We require only the animal."

The fox looked from one to the other to establish their exact positions. No one had any weapons or wands out. Her ability to fox out in a near-instant might grant her the surprise she needed to flee, but Omni couldn't move with her fox speed. She could carry him, but she would need her hands free if she did have to fight anyone.

Damn it. If I go for my phone, the bland mob here will probably rush me. Damn it. I should have called Tahir when I had the chance. That's what I get for assuming there'd be only one freak to deal with.

"Who are you?" she asked. "I deal with a lot of weirdness in my job, but I'm not used to strange men in suits showing up in the middle of the night demanding that women give them their pets. That's a new low." She shrugged. "Maybe a new high."

The man tilted his head a few times, an odd and slightly irritating movement. "The government."

"The government? What about it?"

He gestured around at his clone-like comrades. "We're with the government—a particular agency."

She snorted. "What agency exactly?"

"That is…classified." It still unsettled her how much his voice was like the other man's, lacking any real inflection or emotion. There was something frustrating about being lied to by a man who sounded like he didn't care at all about what he said.

"Sure." Hana rolled her eyes. "You're part of a mysterious government agency that shows up in the middle of the night in Seattle and can't be bothered to explain who you are before demanding people turn their dogs over. I don't believe you. Alison has numerous government contacts, and if you were really were from a government agency, somebody would have put in a request for her help. You're lying, and you've not even done a good job of it."

The man shook his head. "Perhaps you are confused. Let me be clear. The animal you call Omni is not a dog. The shape is but one of many forms it uses as a disguise. That creature is dangerous and a threat to public safety. I must request, for the safety of the people of Seattle, that you surrender Omni to us."

She frowned. "Maybe I'd believe you if you had some kind of badge or identification to show me. Any group of losers can buy identical suits and get identical haircuts, and I'm not confused about the fact that you're all weird."

"Our agency doesn't rely on that kind of thing, but you can trust that we only have the safety of the public in mind." He gestured to Omni. "That is a dangerous creature. We suffered a transportation issue with it. There's no necessity to harm you in its recovery, but we must take it. This is not negotiable. We show mercy in not eliminating you for exposure to the creature."

"No necessity to harm me? Show mercy by not eliminating me?" Hana replied. "Do you even listen to yourself when you talk? Besides the whole creepy no-emotion voice, it's not exactly like you're saying you're good guys. You sound like ruthless killers right now."

"We have to protect the worlds from dangerous creatures, do we not?" The man stared at Omni. "Isn't that what you do, Miss Sugimoto—protect your city? Do not interfere with our recovery. Your safety can't be guaranteed nor is it considered even particularly important."

Okay, I've tried to talk to those jerks, but they seem obsessed with being annoying.

She dropped Omni's leash. It was obvious now that they wouldn't walk out of there without someone's teeth rearranged, and she strongly preferred it was the creeps' around her rather than her own. They made a mistake in not having their weapons out.

"I'm not exactly a non-dangerous woman myself." The fox summoned her tails and grew her claws. She hoped her vulpine eyes would be more intimidating to the freak squad, but given their complete and utter lack of reaction, she doubted it. "And if you attempt to take my pet, I don't know if I can guarantee your safety since I don't believe a single word you've said." She offered the crowd her most dangerous grin.

Predictably, they didn't react.

"You would defend this dangerous creature?" Their spokesman shook his head. "This isn't unexpected by our estimates, but we suspect you do not understand its true nature, even if you understand some of its lesser powers."

"You want me to give Omni up?" She raised her claws.

"That would be the most preferred course of action, yes. I thought that was clear. Do not make this hard on yourself."

"Then you can let me call someone and we can run a little truth spell on you. If you're telling the truth and you want Omni because he's some dangerous creature who might hurt people, I'll consider giving him up. Honestly, you guys come off like creeper assholes, so I have no reason to trust you otherwise. That seems fair, doesn't it?"

Her opponent shook his head. "Fairness is irrelevant in this situation. Our orders don't include maximum preservation of life, yours or otherwise. Consider this your final warning. Any further defiance at this point will end with your possible death or injury. We might also consider capturing an innocent third-party to force your compliance. Our estimates suggest such a strategy would produce a high probability of success."

"Screw you, asshole. Whatever tiny little chance that I believed you guys weren't complete asses just went up in smoke." Hana crouched, ready to launch herself into a sprint at the suited men. "This is your last warning. Get the hell out of here before I shred you."

"Very well, then." The man backed away. "I see reason is ineffective with you. Force will be necessary."

Hana waited for them to produce guns or wands. Several reached into their pockets, but not all. The speaker, along with the others with their hands in their pockets, withdrew a small mass of spiky black crystals, each about the width of a quarter.

She glanced from the man to Omni, totally bewildered. Some kind of explosive artifact maybe? If that were the case, all she needed to do was close the distance so they couldn't use it.

The men with the crystals all opened their mouths and tossed them down their throats before they swallowed. A thick lump was visible as it descended down their throats.

Hana grimaced and her throat twitched in sympathetic

pain. "Okay, that wasn't what I expected at all, and like, ouch! You'll practically need surgery after that."

"All who are not about to fight, focus on keeping the target in sight at all times. The others are to eliminate Hana Sugimoto."

The fox watched her adversaries and frowned. "You'll need much more than—" She gagged when the strange mixed scent of magic and mystery from before choked the air.

The faces and hands of the men who swallowed the crystals twitched violently. Their veins darkened and the tangible spread took several seconds. Their eyes turned solid black.

"Okay, definitely weird, but not exactly the stuff of terror," she insisted. "So you have some kind of crazy transformation crystal, but I'm still me, and you're still boring old you."

The leader attacked, his movement almost a blur. No normal human could run that fast.

Okay, the world's deadliest lozenge gave you powers, but it won't be enough against my natural weapons.

Hana sprinted away from Omni and ducked low to swipe her claws across the man's chest.

They ripped through his suit and shirt and she gasped when she scored his skin and a loud scraping sound followed. Although she drew blood, her claws didn't sink deeply. It was like trying to cut through metal. Apparently, the world's deadliest lozenge also granted armor.

The man backhanded her and the blow catapulted her away. She landed in the moist mud pit that passed for the lawn and rolled a few times before she scrambled to her feet and wiped the blood off her mouth.

"Okay, I'll give you that one, but now, I know the deal." The fox surged toward the speaker and this time, raked across his face. He grunted and stumbled back. That gave her an opening to hack at his throat. Shallow wounds gave way to deep gouges and he tottered as blood spurted from his neck. He fell to his knees and held his hands to the wound, but his face still stubbornly displayed not even a hint of any real emotion.

Who the hell are these guys? No one's that disciplined. It's like he can't even feel fear.

Hana's heart thundered even harder as if to make up for the lack of emotion displayed by her enemies. In a world of magic, some things still remained unnatural. This wasn't like fighting the waterlings. These men could talk and were alive and aware. They should at least have had the decency to act worried or afraid when they were dying.

Several others launched an attack. They were faster than normal humans but not quite as fast as she was in her current form. Now that she knew their capabilities, she could adjust for them. She sidestepped the first attack, slashed across the back neck of one of the enemy, and managed to draw blood. When she spun for a follow-up attack, another man kicked her in the back. The hard blow shoved her face-first into the ground and she exhaled another hissed breath when pain radiated from her back.

I would kill for my tachi *about now. I bet it would slice through these bastards easier.*

She leapt to her feet and swiped viciously at the closest opponent. This time, she achieved a far deeper ragged incision from stomach to neck than she had against the leader. The man didn't cry out and instead, uttered a quiet grunt as he fell. She pounced on another assailant nearby and dug into his throat.

I can do this. I only have to disable enough of them.

About half the men had transformed. The remainder simply stood and did absolutely nothing—like it was some boring school play they were forced to watch. She doubted that they could withstand her claws as well as their changed friends could. That gave her an idea. It was time for a little distraction and a chance to limit potential reinforcements at the same time.

The fox raced toward one of the unchanged men, but another who had transformed barreled into her side and knocked her down. She stabbed into his chest with her claws several times until she finally pierced deep. Blood spewed and she yanked her claws out and pushed him down. It was hard to fight when your heart had several new holes in it.

Smug victory thoughts should wait. She realized that when another attacker came up from behind her and punched her in the back of the head.

She grunted in pain and fell to her hands and knees, her vision swimming. Three of the transformed men surrounded her and began to pummel and kick her. She threw up her arms to block but their blows continued to rain down on her like three angry sledgehammers. Pain consumed her body and consciousness.

Shit. I hope Omni escaped. I didn't pay attention to him in the fight. I don't know what he really is, but I'm damned sure these bastards shouldn't have him.

Hana fell awkwardly. Her left arm throbbed and the intense pain almost overwhelmed her, and she was sure it was broken. She slumped and grass and mud half-filled her mouth.

"If I had my sword," she began and coughed blood from the effort. "I would have killed all of you, and I still killed several of you despite your stupid crystal of power."

One of her adversaries looked at the downed leader, her first victim. The man's hands had fallen away from his throat, and although his eyes were open, he'd obviously stopped breathing. Blood coated his suit from his neck wound.

At least the bastards don't regenerate.

The other man knelt and placed his palm on the dead leader's head. When he withdrew it, there was a small trickle of blood from the middle of the dead man's forehead that hadn't been there before.

Some sort of ritual, or did he actually do something to him? I doubt he did it simply for fun.

He stood and turned toward her. "You accomplished nothing, Hana Sugimoto. If you had handed the creature over, we would have been more inclined to allow your survival, although your elimination was likely necessary anyway. You have seen too much."

She coughed up more blood and fought the darkness that clawed at the edge of her vision as she sprawled motionless, hot pain rampant in her body. "Hey, dope. You know what I don't see?"

"No. I cannot see through your eyes. Your question has no point."

"No, it has a point. The answer is simple. Omni." Hana

managed a pained grin. "He probably turned into a bird and flew away, so big deal if you kill me." She groaned as a slight movement sent a shockwave of pain from her arm through her body. "You can kill me, but the whole reason you showed up is gone."

The man looked around, his movements jerky. "Confirm. Is the target in sight?"

His companions began to look for Omni.

"We have lost sight of the target," one declared. "Transformation likely. All Strands prepare for additional battle."

The now familiar scent of Omni's transformation magic drifted into Hana's nose. "Good boy. Get out of here. Mommy wasn't strong enough to protect you."

An unearthly growl filled the air. The men all halted in place.

CHAPTER SIXTEEN

The attackers backed away from the noise to form a rough semi-circle. The untransformed men drew their guns. Although their speed of movement betrayed concern, their expressions remained as neutral and utterly expressionless as before.

So they were holding out because they didn't think they needed it. I'm kind of pissed, but I'd probably be dead already if they hadn't. I can only dodge so much, and now I remember how vulnerable I am without one of the defensive artifacts.

"The target can survive heavy damage," the second leader announced. "Do what is necessary."

Hana blinked and rolled onto her side to look in the direction of the growl. The noise sounded like it came from a copse of nearby trees.

Moments later, a tall, thin, dark creature, easily seven feet tall, emerged from the trees. A hard, dark carapace covered its lumbering form. Its arms ended in four sharp claws, and its four dark eyes sat in the center of its squat, triangular head, which possessed only the thinnest slit for a mouth. A short tail covered in the same material twitched loosely behind it. Several seconds passed before she realized it raced directly toward her.

And I had such a good couple of weeks. Wait. Could this be... They said... No, it couldn't be. It's too big.

She groaned when the pain of her injuries began to win the war against the adrenaline that barely kept her conscious. The pain clouded her mind and made it hard to think, but she was desperate to remain aware. With no one there to use a healing potion on her, if she didn't force herself to stay awake, she risked death. That was assuming the emotionless assholes in suits didn't finish off the creature now rushing toward them.

The suited men opened fire simultaneously in a perfectly coordinated volley. The cloud of bullets struck the creature and sparked before they bounced off its thick carapace with no apparent damage. The combined muzzle flashes were almost beautiful in a way, a small explosion of deadly art in the middle of the night.

The monster picked up the pace, inconvenienced at best by the gunshots. It wasn't bleeding, nor had it slowed or showed any evidence that it had been more than scratched by the concerted firepower.

I wonder if those are anti-magic bullets.

Hana bit her lip and waited to get torn apart. She drew some small satisfaction from the fact that at least the jerks would go down too. The creature rocketed past her and impaled one of the armored men closest to her with its claw. It pushed all the way through until the claw came out the other side.

The victim shuddered violently and began to crumble

into small particles that flowed directly into his killer. The odd process hollowed out the clothes until they fell, the body now gone and completely absorbed by the creature.

Okay, am I seeing what I think I'm seeing, or am I losing it because every part of me hurts?

She blinked several times as the empty clothes fluttered into an untidy heap. Now that the monster was closer to both her and a light pole, she could make out that it wasn't black like she initially suspected, but a familiar dark brown —the identical shade as Omni.

The conclusion was inescapable. Omni might normally only be able to keep his same small size, but suddenly, he'd become big, scary, and angry. Despite her pain, Hana loved it. The fact that he ignored her—an easy target on the ground—and targeted the men proved that he wasn't a wild, out-of-control killing machine like others suggested or that Alison and the others were worried about. He was still her fur-feather-scale baby, only a little bigger and badder at the moment, and she needed that.

"You get them, boy," she called. "You show these assholes not to mess with us." She groaned and shook her head slowly in an effort to clear her vision.

The original leader had ordered the men to keep their eyes on Omni. That meant that they understood that he couldn't change while being directly watched, but some-how, in the chaos of the fight, people had let their attention wander and so gave the pet the chance he needed.

If at least one of those assholes had done his job, this would already be over. They could simply stuff him in a glass case or something.

More of the transformed agents swarmed Omni and

delivered a relentless barrage of punches and kicks. The deadly blows that had shattered her bones bounced off the carapace and made little impression. The beast didn't seem to notice them and simply attacked whoever was closest.

Hana's claws might have had difficulty piercing the hardened skin of their odd assailants, but Omni's sliced into them with ease. Their enhanced skin provided no more apparent resistance than it normally would against a sharp blade. The creature killed three of his opponents in a matter of seconds, including decapitating one man, but he took a moment to absorb each man like he'd done with his first kill. Two of the remaining armored men leapt toward him, the height of their jump impressive. He simply snatched both out of the air and pounded them into each other before he absorbed them.

Despite his initial growl, he hadn't made any other noises during his killing spree. No growls, hisses, or satisfied chirps or buzzes, only the sickening sounds of the claws. His adversaries, too, were surprisingly quiet and uttered no screams or yells or begged for mercy, only the occasional grunt. Their expressions remained unchanged even as the tall, unearthly monster continued to slaughter them.

The untransformed men ceased their fire and exchanged hasty looks. One of them glanced at the now dead second commander before they all holstered their weapons and turned to flee. Omni managed to snag one before he could escape and his claws decimated him, but he tossed the body to the ground rather than absorb it.

Does he feed off that crystal stuff or something? I wonder if he's been hungry since I don't feed him anything but normal pet food.

Hana crawled forward, the effort accompanied by hisses of pain. The gunfire might bring the police and ambulances, but she wasn't sure if she wanted them to come and start asking the inevitable questions. She rolled onto her back and made a feeble attempt to reach for a healing potion in her pocket. Her hand wouldn't move the right way and agony seared through her.

One of her arms was completely shattered, and the pain from that injury had masked the fact that her other wrist was broken. She released a strangled laugh at the realization that she had the powerful potion she needed to heal her injuries but she couldn't reach it.

If I die in a park, I'll be totally embarrassed, especially since it was the suit patrol that did it. They aren't cool enough to be the people responsible for killing Hot Fox.

Their assailants had already all but vanished from sight as they raced away but lingered for a moment at the edge of her vision. The dark suits blended naturally into the darkness and left her and Omni alone with several piles of empty clothes and dead bodies. Given her condition, their ambush had almost been successful.

The creature moved to Hana and stood over her. He leaned down and picked her up, his movements gentle and considerate compared to the massacre delivered only moments before. She tried not to notice that he was covered in the blood of his victims.

"Fox and the hound for the win." Hana took a few shuddering breaths. "Thanks, boy. I wish you could have done that earlier, but I understand that you're shy about changing when people are watching." She managed a smile and coughed another bloody mouthful. "You need to get me home unless you know how to get the potion out of my pocket and give it to me. I...I... Sorry...I have trouble keeping my eyes open. Don't hurt any cops who come. If they shoot at you, run away or hide and turn into something cute."

She groaned and finally lost the fight against the darkness.

CHAPTER SEVENTEEN

Alison sighed. The last thing she wanted to do on date night was stand in a parking garage wrapped in an invisibility spell waiting for assassins to appear, but that's how the night had gone.

Her original plan was to stand beside a Chevy—her Dad's prejudices had somehow manifested in her behavior —but Mason made it clear that they should stay near her car. That was most likely where whoever was following them would look once they realized they had lost sight of their quarry. They both wove a few minor anti-tracking wards—not enough to stop serious efforts but at least enough that they would likely know if someone used magic to search for them.

"This sucks," she muttered. "And I can't shake the feeling that these aren't merely some idiots from the Eastern Union or Vargas' hitmen."

"You think so?" He shrugged. "I saw them. The more I think about it, the more I wonder if they weren't trying to actually be careful."

"Yeah, you saw them." She frowned. "But I didn't, so they were being careful enough."

He winked. "Being a bodyguard originally rather than a bounty hunter has its advantages at times. I think you're still obsessed with hunting people rather than being hunted. It's why we make such a great team, A."

"Maybe." She folded her arms and tapped her foot. It was annoying not being able to see herself or her boyfriend while they talked. They'd waited there for twenty minutes already. Their pursuers were either lazy or they had lost them. "I wonder what this is about. There are too many people on a growing list of people I have pissed off. Sometimes, it's weird not knowing who might be coming to kill you."

Yeah, I see what Carla was getting at. When Dad was hunted by Harriken or assassins, I was safe at the School of Necessary Magic. But if I have a kid, they won't be a high-schooler ready to be sent off to a magical boarding school, and things like waiting to ambush people following you during date night aren't all that compatible with a stable family life.

Then again, it's not like Mom and Dad have totally given up their old jobs. She's not doing any raids while she's pregnant, but he hasn't even bothered to keep it that low key since she got pregnant.

"Got them," Mason murmured. "They're coming our way."

Alison looked around since she couldn't see him and where he was looking. The clack of footfalls echoed with increasing loudness as a half-dozen almost identical men in dark suits marched up the stairs and onto the concrete parking area. They glanced around for a moment before they strode toward Alison's car. None carried any obvious weapons, but they could hide a decent-sized wand or gun in their suit jackets.

"I won't let them hurt the Spider," she declared. "Are you ready? We have the surprise here."

"We can't kill them without knowing who they are."

"I know that," she replied. "I'm hoping simply the fact that we have the drop on them will convince them they've already lost this one, but we'll see."

"Ladies first," he murmured in response. "I'll try to avoid hitting your car."

"Very funny." She layered a shield over herself and extended a shadow blade. The combined magical effects disrupted the spell hiding her. The six men turned, tilted their heads at the same angle and same time, and looked vaguely curious but not angry, concerned, threatened or, for that matter, even vaguely surprised.

"Yeah, that's not creepy at all," she observed and pointed her blade at them. "Okay, you've followed us around tonight, so let's hear the spiel about how you'll kill the Dark Princess, blah, blah, and show your power. I assume this is some feeble assassination attempt." She flicked the wrist of her free hand. "Or we can cut to the chase, and I can explain how I'll defeat you and that this is pointless. You don't want me as an enemy. Trust me. You really don't. I don't even have to know who you are to tell you that."

Mason took the opportunity to cast his own shield spell before he activated his strength and speed spells. The six men didn't react at all and the same neutral expression masked their faces. Even if they couldn't sense the magic, his obvious movements and incantations should have tipped them off.

What do they know that we don't? They haven't reacted much, and they also haven't tried to stop us from preparing for a fight.

One of the men stepped forward, his arms at his sides. There was nothing particularly noteworthy about him compared with the others. They weren't sextuplets, but she wouldn't have been surprised if they were related.

Is that what who they are? Some weird magical family or something?

"We don't desire trouble with you, Alison Brownstone," the man explained, his voice flat and devoid of any hint of feeling. "We feel engaging you in battle would be a fruitless expenditure of resources for little gain. You currently only incidentally threaten our goals."

"Then you can back the hell off," she suggested. "But not before you tell me who you are. I don't appreciate creepy guys stalking me when I'm on a date."

The team spread out with no tension at all on their faces. They were either delusional or very brave.

"You do not need to know who we are at this moment." Their apparent leader nodded. "Everything we do is for the betterment of this world. That might not immediately be clear, but we can assure you of that. Myopia may cause some to not understand that, but it's not our concern."

"Many tyrants who butcher millions on their way to consolidating power claim they do it for a better world." Alison scoffed. She lowered her arm but didn't release the magic fueling her shadow blade. She wanted the men to understand that she could attack them at any moment. "So

I have no reason to believe anything you weird and suspicious guys who have followed me around have to say in that regard. You don't exactly give off a hardened criminal vibe, but there is a rich tapestry of twisted bastards out there."

The man stared at Alison and for the first time, something almost approaching actual feeling appeared on his face. "Your belief is unnecessary," he replied. He turned toward Mason. "Neither of your beliefs are necessary. Only your compliance in this situation."

"Our compliance?" She narrowed her eyes. "I don't get it. If you don't want trouble with me, why are you trawling the city in a big pack looking for me? Somehow, I doubt it's because you all really, really like me and want my autograph."

"We needed to secure your presence." He shrugged. "But only for a limited time. We are now doing that. You are complying with our goals."

Mason frowned. "What do you mean by that? You're stalling us?"

"An appropriate description. Don't worry. We anticipate our business with you will be over very soon. Our estimates suggest a high probability of success. We apologize for the inconvenience, but we can't risk your interference with our overall operation."

Alison grew a pair of shadow wings. Sometimes, flashier spells made for better intimidation.

"You're really starting to piss me off." She gritted her teeth for a moment to regain a calm tone. "And I don't like the fact that you're hanging around my car and talking about deliberately stalling us. That means you're up to something you know I wouldn't like, and I'm beginning to think I should simply carve through you and fly up to see what trouble you've caused."

"Battling us would be pointless," the man insisted. "And you will not be able to see anything from flying around this area."

"Pointless? Why? Because we'd eliminate you in three seconds?"

"Any conflict with you in this parking garage will likely result in high casualties on our side. That has been taken into account for all operational estimates. It's as I told you. We're not here to engage in battle." He shrugged and gestured around the space and at the different types of cars and trucks parked within. "All our intelligence suggests this tactical environment would favor you, but we can engage here in a way that will delay your escape from this area."

She marched forward, but the men didn't move. "Get out of my way, or I'll teach you a little something about compliance."

"We will leave," her opponent insisted with an easy shrug. "When we receive orders to that effect."

"Who gives the orders?" Mason asked, his wand still pointed at the men.

"You don't need to know that information at this time. A superior gives the orders. Our goal is to carry out those orders."

"Well, aren't you the good little soldier?" She studied the odd team quickly. They had made no attempt to arm themselves. She sensed some light magic from them, but not as much as she would have suspected. Unless they had a spectacular surprise, she could lay them out without too much trouble.

A light buzzing noise sounded. Alison raised her blade, ready to defend herself. The leader raised his arm to look at his watch.

"I will kill you if necessary," she threatened.

"That will not be necessary." The man turned to the others. "Retreat. Losses against Alison Brownstone are now considered unacceptable."

His comrades nodded in response, and the entire group of six slowly retreated, their attention still fixed on the couple.

"That's right." She brandished her blade. "Congratulations for not being idiots, but whoever you are and whatever this is about doesn't end today. I'll find out who you are, and we'll finish the discussion about why you were following us."

"All actions have consequences. Your suggested plan is logical." The emotionless reply startled her for a moment, and she let it slide.

Mason walked to her side, his wand still in his hand but not pointed at the men.

The team reached the stairs and finally turned their backs as they jogged down. They still didn't betray any fear or concern.

Alison's face twisted in disgust. "Okay, I don't know who those guys were, but they are creepy. And what was with always referring to me as 'Alison Brownstone?'"

He shrugged. "What's so weird about that? It's your name."

"I don't call you Mason Lind every time I refer to you

directly. It's weird." She shook her head. "I don't know...the way they said it made my skin crawl, and we still don't know who they are."

"Do you regret letting them walk?"

She shook her head. "I don't know enough about their capabilities to risk a big fight here. For all I know, they'll self-destruct like that revenant and bring this entire parking garage down. If someone's smart enough to back off when I tell them to back off, that's a good thing. We can investigate and then take the fight to them."

Her phone rang. She fished around in her pocket to locate it. The call was from Tahir.

"Good timing," she answered. "We had the weirdest run-in with some freaks."

"Then I would call that rather suspicious timing," he responded. "Or worrisome."

Alison frowned. "What do you mean?"

"I can't get hold of Hana. She sent me a text about taking Omni for a walk, but when I got home, she was still gone and hasn't answered her phone." Tension infused his voice. "I also can't track her or her phone. I'm currently searching the neighborhood visually with drones."

She closed her eyes and took a deep breath. "Damn it. That explains it."

"Explains what?" the infomancer demanded.

"I thought we scared off the guys who followed us, but they basically told us their plan. They were here to stall us, probably while they targeted Hana, who was conveniently with Omni. I imagine they were even deliberately chatty because they thought that would delay us longer than fighting. The timing is too perfect." She shook her head. "I think whoever sent that message to you about Omni made their move. Mason and I are on our way. Maybe a ritual will help with tracking."

"What if...that's no longer useful?" Tahir asked, his voice tight.

Alison drew a deep breath and released it slowly and her heart pounded even harder than it had during her confrontation. She refused to believe Hana was dead.

"If you're saying what I think you're saying, we'll identify who is behind it and we'll make them wish they were only Harriken," she stated coldly.

"But the Harriken were annihilated," he replied.

"Exactly. We'll be there soon." She nodded to Mason. "Let's go." As she hung up, the phone buzzed with a text from Drysi addressed to her, Mason, Tahir, and Hana.

Some men were following me, but they backed off suddenly. Have no bloody clue who they were. I don't think they were drunken hooligans, but they didn't come off as pros, either.

She gritted her teeth. At this point, she wouldn't have been surprised to learn the men in suits had caused several traffic accidents to keep the team away from their friend.

CHAPTER EIGHTEEN

Hana groaned and blinked several times, reluctant to open her eyes. Cold...she felt so very cold. She'd always suspected she would die young but getting beaten to death by weird crystal-munchers in suits didn't even crack her top ten of likely deaths.

A little snicker escaped. It was an odd list, since it included things like number five, getting crushed by the Fremont Troll in Mountain Strider mode.

I hope I didn't reincarnate as something totally ugly. I know that's petty, but if I can't come back as a fox or a human, maybe at least a cool animal—a cat, maybe. Then again, maybe I ended up in a hell or I'm a platypus.

Hey. I can still think. That's a good sign. I'm not a grubworm or a germ or something.

Something soft and furry rubbed against her thigh, and she opened her eyes. Omni lay beside her, not in his deadly, hulking form but instead, as an adorable small brown cat. He purred and pushed his head against her hand. She was propped up against the trunk of a pine tree, still very much a nine-tailed fox in her humanoid form and not a grub-worm, a cat, or a platypus.

"Sweet. I'm not dead. Everything's going Sugimoto." She licked her lips and looked around. "I think this is the same park." Cautiously, she moved her arms. "Huh, and I don't hurt. That's a nice bonus." She blinked. "Why don't I hurt? Those guys beat me like bratty toddlers going after the same doll, but I don't feel any pain at all."

Omni backed away from her and pawed at something on the ground. It was hard to make out what it was in the dim light, so she fumbled until she managed to grab what turned out to be an empty potion vial—specifically her empty healing potion.

"I don't remember taking this. I only remember passing out." Her gaze returned to Omni. "Did you give it to me?"

He purred.

She stroked his fur gently. "Mommy loves you, too." She stood and stretched before she dug in her pocket for her phone. The healing potion had brought her back from the brink of death, but it couldn't do anything for the pulverized mass of metal, pink plastic, and glass that used to be her phone. She was so used to having shielding that she never even considered what might happen to it in a fight. "I'm glad I didn't bring my new purse for the walk. Those assholes would have destroyed it."

Omni wandered between her legs and looked at her.

Hana held up the destroyed device. "And they said this was supposed to be a rugged case. It couldn't even take a few magically enhanced freaks pounding hard enough to break bone? I should ask for my money back. It was cute, though. Too bad." She stuck it back in her pocket. "New plan. If any new crystal munchers show up, I'll run around in circles until you can go into a bush and turn into Angry Omni, and then you can suck their souls or whatever it is you do." She winked at the animal. "For now, we should get home. I'll have Alison handle the questions the cops have about all the bodies we left behind. I'm sure we can track these freaks and find out who they are. Because I know one thing, I didn't like them trying to grab you before, and I don't like them after they tried to kill me."

Omni meowed loudly.

Alison soared over the park, her earbud receiver active. "I've found the bloodstains you saw with the drones, Tahir. It's weird. I've passed over them a few times, and they're getting smaller. I also don't see any bodies. Someone definitely wanted to keep the area clean."

"The police received reports of gunfire from that vicinity," Tahir cautioned. "But I've rerouted them so we can handle the issue ourselves."

You mean get our revenge if we find Hana dead. Fair enough. It's not like I wasn't thinking the same thing.

"Any sign of our business-class friends?"

He responded with something approaching a growl of frustration. "I've not located any brown-haired men in suits in the area. I'll set up additional algorithms for the cameras and drones once we find Hana. These men will not escape."

"I wouldn't worry too much about finding them," she replied. "I suspect that whoever they are and whatever happened tonight, this is far from our last run-in with them, but you're right. The most important thing at the moment is to find Hana and get her home. We can decide where to go from there once we've accomplished that."

"Agreed."

Alison widened her search circle and dropped closer to the ground. She could clearly see where a battle had taken place, although the evidence continued to slowly disappear.

Is this pointless? Even the direct tracking spell with one of Hana's hairs didn't work. We might be wasting time looking for her in this park when they have her locked in a warded barge at the docks or they've already tossed her through a portal to Oriceran.

She gritted her teeth in frustration. For all her strength and power, she couldn't find her best friend in a park near her home. She vowed right then and there, if Hana was dead, she would do everything in her power and call in every favor to find the organization that did it and burn them out of existence. That might not be the Brownstone Effect, but it was definitely the Brownstone Solution.

This is what Carla doesn't understand. This is what we deal with—not only a few thugs here and there but deadly and powerful people who will stop at nothing to achieve their goals. The government is still playing catchup, and until they can, people like me and Dad are necessary to fill the gap. Otherwise, evil assholes will think they can do whatever they want on Earth.

Alison was about to turn for another pass when something dark and humanoid emerged from the trees. She summoned a shadow blade, ready to attack any suited bastard she saw. She flew lower and exhaled a gasp of relief as the figure stepped into the illumination of a lamppost.

Hana marched toward the sidewalk, a brown cat near her feet who had to be Omni. "I have eyes on her. She's alive." She took a few deep breaths.

"You do?" Tahir sounded shocked. "I wonder why I wasn't able to track her. You didn't give her an anti-tracking artifact, did you? One that you perhaps forget to mention."

"Nope. I assume it probably has something to do with Omni. We already know it's hard to track him, so maybe he can extend it to others." She flew toward the woman, who waved as soon as she noticed her. She landed gently and released her wings in front of her friend.

The fox's coat and clothes were torn and bloodstained. She'd obviously been in a major fight. All the vanishing blood wasn't an illusion.

"You look like you were in a slap fight with a bear and lost," Alison commented and examined her with narrowed eyes. "What the hell happened?"

"Some weirdoes in suits showed up." Hana nodded toward the cat. "And they wanted Omni. They claimed to be from some secret government agency and insisted he was some super-dangerous creature they needed to capture. I told them to screw off, and we fought." She shrugged. "It got pretty intense. I wonder if the police would get mad if I walked around with the *tachi* all the time. It would have been nice."

"Weirdoes in suits seems to be the theme of the night." She took a step forward and hugged her tightly. "We thought we'd lost you. Seriously, you have no idea how glad I am to see you. Not only is my best friend still alive, but now, I don't have to launch a campaign of bloody vengeance." She forced a smile. "That's really more a spring or summer thing."

"Yeah, I agree. Winter's supposed to be for brooding and planning." Hana patted her back. "It's okay. I thought I'd lost myself for a minute." She pulled away with a weary smile. "The suit idiots...I don't know how to explain it. Some of them ate this weird spiky crystal thing, and it changed them—made them faster and tougher. I killed a few of them, but I didn't have my artifacts or my sword, so they kicked the crap out of me. I thought I was done for. It's a long time since I've been that messed up."

Alison nodded. "What happened? Did they simply leave? That's what happened with the guys who followed Mason and I and Drysi. They all suddenly left. We thought—"

"You thought they left because they killed me and got what they wanted?"

"Yeah, basically." She shrugged and sighed.

The fox shook her head. "Nope. They didn't leave. They ran." She grinned at Omni. "It turns out my little fur-feather-scale baby has another secret. He escaped in the scuffle, and he came back big, angry, and lethal. Exactly what they were looking for, I suppose, but not what they wanted to see."

"Wait, but he doesn't really change size, right?" She frowned. "How dangerous can he be at that size? Even if he turned into a wolverine or something?"

"Nope, this time, he was like..." Hana frowned in thought and her tongue stuck out the side of her mouth. "It was weird. I smelled magic but other stuff, too, from both those guys and maybe Omni. The way he looked reminded me vaguely...I don't know, maybe the armor your dad wears, to be honest. Not exactly like that—it was a different color and material, but strong. He was bullet-proof and super-tough, and...uh, walking upright. Like armor, but still organic. Does that make sense?"

Alison stared at Omni and swallowed.

Shit.

She had waited for the right time to tell her friends the truth about her father—that he was a non-Oriceran extraterrestrial, not with a magical amulet but an intelligent, adaptive biotech symbiont thousands of years more advanced than Earth technology. While Hana's simple description made it clear that Omni wasn't a Vax like her father, the mere fact that the fox's mind even went there suggested the mysterious pet might have non-Oriceran alien connections too.

That would bring a whole host of other complications, particularly from the government. Even if James had destroyed some of the more vicious alien-hunting factions, there were many men in dark suits and three-letter agencies that didn't want non-Oriceran aliens walking free.

Wait. Hana smelled magic, and we all sense magic from Omni when he changes. All those Nine Systems Alliances aliens who've attacked Dad made it clear they haven't seen magic anywhere in the galaxy but Earth and Oriceran. That means Omni can't possibly be an alien, right?

She nodded slowly. "So, he is dangerous enough to kill men strong enough to defeat us."

"I should point out that it's only because they surprised

me, outnumbered me, and outgeared me, and I still gave them a hell of a fight." Hana rolled her eyes. "As for Omni, he's only dangerous to jerks who try to kill his mommy. I don't know who those guys are, but if they're government agents, I'm a nun."

Alison gestured into the distance toward the path and grass where she'd seen the bloodstains. "Is that where you fought them?"

He friend nodded. "Yeah, but..." She looked around, clearly confused. "I killed several of them. Omni did, too. Some of them, he kind of...I don't know how to explain it...absorbed, but I saw him kill at least one. Where are the bodies? Did the cops come?"

She shook her head. "Nope. No cops. And that's the big question. Where are the bodies? These freaks didn't want to stand and fight while Omni did his best angry Brownstone impression, but they risked coming back to collect their dead guys? The bloodstains are slowly disappearing, too. I sense mild magic so it could be a spell."

"Maybe it's a no soldier left behind type thing." The fox shrugged.

"Or they don't want to leave behind too many samples that could be subjected to magical or genetic testing." She frowned. "I'm not surprised that Omni had another trick up his sleeve, but we still don't know much about him, and more to the point, we don't know who the hell is hunting him."

CHAPTER NINETEEN

The next morning, the main team gathered in the conference room, including Ava. Sonya was helping Jerry's team with a minor job, and everyone agreed it would be best for the girl to have time to process what had happened with her father before she was introduced to more deadly secrets. She might be a talented and intelligent magical, but she was still a young girl learning who she was in the world.

Omni lay at Hana's feet, curled up in dog form, and snored contentedly.

Alison glanced at the animal.

He looks cute and non-threatening, but he turned into a killing machine less than twelve hours ago. Is he some kind of biological weapon? If I even dare to suggest that, Hana would try to cut my head off, but at the same time, she's right. If he was a weapon, he had more than enough opportunity to go rampant. Maybe he's merely the ultimate guard dog.

Ava eyed the animal with a faint hint of disdain. "Are

you certain about this, Miss Brownstone? Have you considered all the implications?"

Everyone had already shared their notes about what had happened the night before, and the woman had taken careful notes on the three different encounters.

Alison shrugged. "This is the safest place for Omni. Whoever those suit guys are, they won't risk a frontal attack on Brownstone Security. Not only do we have heavy defenses, but it's too easy for AET to get here quickly. If they thought they could win head-on against the entire team, they wouldn't have used three different teams the other night."

"That's true, and I agree with your analysis, but that's not what I'm talking about."

"What do you mean, then?"

Her assistant adjusted the wireframe glasses perched on her nose. "I'm less concerned about the more tactical implications of Omni being present as opposed to the direct impact on personnel policy here. You made it very clear before that you didn't want people to bring their pets to work for both safety and hygiene reasons. Unless you're willing to admit to the entire company that Omni isn't a normal pet, you risk people raising protests of favoritism and hypocrisy. That will affect morale, even if it doesn't result in direct challenges to authority. I'm sure more than a few of our employees would love to bring their pets."

She chuckled. Leave it to her administrative assistant to focus on the basic impact on the business. Sometimes, she forgot that she was running an entire company and not merely the small elite magical team. Occasionally, she worked closely with Jerry's team, but for the most part, they handled more conventional threats and jobs, while her team focused on crazed crystal-eating men in suits and dangerous government projects running amok.

"For now, the official story is Omni's very sick," she explained. "And so this is a mercy thing. If anyone wants to talk to me about bringing in their very sick pets, I'll approve it on a case-by-case basis, but make it clear to people we haven't become a pet-friendly company, if only for their safety. I can't guarantee that no one will ever attack this place again. There's always someone out there who thinks they can succeed in a surprise attack."

"Of course, Miss Brownstone." Ava nodded and tapped a few notes into her tablet.

"That brings us back to our friends from last night," she continued with a shrug. "We know what they want—Omni —but that's not the same thing as knowing why they want him or who they are. Given everything they said to different people last night and their general attitudes, I don't buy their claims for a second. It's unlikely that they're only trying to protect everyone, which means whatever they want him for is probably something that might actually hurt people."

"Perhaps," Ava suggested, "there's another possibility."

"What's that?"

"Their goal might be neutral, as it were, even if their methods are vicious and criminal." She nodded to Hana. "When she specialized in confidence scams and trickery, her fundamental goal was simply survival. Although her activities were criminal and involved taking advantage of people, her overall intent wasn't to harm them."

The fox rolled her eyes. "Why do I always have to be the example?"

"Because my shit's far harder to explain away," the Welsh witch muttered.

The assistant stared at Drysi for a moment before she focused on her boss. "I would not risk assuming too much about their long-term motives. Think also of the Seventh Order. They sought domination and control, and it wasn't inherent in their goals that so many people had to die, but they engaged in brutal acts of terrorism and assassination. The ends don't always define the means."

Alison nodded. "True enough. That means we need to gather more information. Tahir, any luck?"

The infomancer shook his head and scowled. "I'm ashamed to admit my efforts keep dead-ending, and strangely, I've not been able to find any of these men. I even checked the parking garage cameras from your encounter, but the cameras malfunctioned. The footage was empty—as in nothing recorded—then there are several minutes of nothing although I could see it running, then there's only you and Mason. It's extremely unlikely the cameras would fail only and exactly during the time period the men were inside without a direct cause related to them."

Mason grimaced. He nodded at Omni. "He has inherent anti-tracking abilities. It's not crazy to believe the men who have targeted him have something similar. For all we know, he's some kind of creation of theirs. That might explain a lot."

"It's not a crazy thought," Alison replied. "But it's damned annoying, and those abilities don't tell us much about who they are other than the fact they want to keep themselves secret. We know they have access to at least some magic and artifacts, including those crystals they ate that transformed them. We also know they are a limited resource."

"How do we know that?" Hana asked.

"Because not all of them used them when they attacked you. The ones who didn't ended up using guns, so it wasn't like they simply held them in reserve."

"Good point."

Tahir nodded. "The available evidence does strongly point away from them being the government, despite what they told Hana. I mostly question their tactics and statements, and even their chosen attack venue."

The fox nodded. "Not that I wouldn't put it past some CIA assassin squad to try to kill someone this sexy because they're fools, but they didn't come off as trained agents. They came off as drugged weirdoes." She shrugged. "Not that I know what a trained CIA agent should act like."

"I agree," Alison replied with a frown. "And both my parents have dealt extensively with government non-magical agents. They use state-of-the-art tech, and they aren't the kind of agents who will stand there and tell you they're deliberately trying to stall you."

"Not only that," Tahir interjected, "but even the deepest black ops of the CIA still have certain control mechanisms and contacts. The government has many reasons to be leery of the Brownstone family. To fling large groups of agents at a close friend of a Brownstone risks the wrath of the entire family."

That's true, and the higher-ups know about Dad. I'll need to ask him soon if I can share his secret. Even though I don't think this situation has anything to do with aliens, I don't like not being able to tell my closest friends the truth. For now, though, them knowing wouldn't help with this situation.

"You're right." She gestured to Omni. "It wasn't all that long ago that we were involved in helping to eliminate a failure from a government-funded project—one they were desperate to cover up, even though it involved innocent people. If these Omni hunters were with the government, Agent Latherby or Senator Johnston would probably have gotten wind of it and one of them would have nudged me toward them."

Mason folded his arms. "What's with the suits and the almost identical looks? Is it supposed to be some kind of fashion statement? Gang regulation?"

"Who knows? If we can't take pictures of them because of their magic or inherent nature, it might be a stealth strategy. In any event, we still have one strong line of evidence. This all goes back to Omni." She blew out an irritated breath. "I think it's time to take this wider than in-house. Even if it's not government, someone there might have a clue. What I mean is, there might be evidence the government has that we could make more sense of. Latherby owes me more than a few favors. I'm sure he can ask around in a quiet way. I don't want to push toward Senator Johnston unless I really need him. He's run a lot of interference for me this last year, and I know it's brought him heat."

Drysi cleared her throat. "I hate to be the right bloody bitch in the room, but we do have to face the obvious. Omni is dangerous, and we still have no fucking clue what he is. Now, we have him here in the building. What if he gets angry, goes into a closet, and comes out and kills half of Jerry's team?" She shrugged. "We don't even know if he can easily be killed in his angry form or if he's vulnerable to particular spells, elements, or anti-magic bullet."

Hana frowned at her. "We don't need to know that because he won't go out of control here and hurt anyone."

"How do you know?" The witch pointed at the dog. "You saw him slaughter men the other night. At the very least, you know he's capable of it, and who knows what he was doing when he was sucking those men in. Maybe he has a taste for human souls now."

Tahir rubbed his chin. "It does imply, perhaps, some relationship between the crystals those men consumed and Omni. A similar magic basis, perhaps? I doubt it has anything to do with simply absorbing souls. Otherwise, he would have disposed of the non-crystal eater's body in the same way."

Drysi didn't look convinced, but she didn't offer any additional comments.

Alison shook her head. "We don't know what any of this means, but I think Hana's right. I don't think Omni's dangerous to us or any of the other Brownstone Security Employees."

Hana nodded. "Damned right I'm right. I always am. Well, mostly am. Right at least half the time."

The witch sighed and shook her head. "I'm sorry. I wasn't trying to get him thrown out."

"It's not that I think what you're saying is unreasonable, Drysi, and I've thought the same thing. But we've only seen him become violent in one very particular situation, which supports the idea that he'll only become violent in similar circumstances. Many normal pets attack people who threaten their owners, and that's often something that's applauded." Alison pointed at Omni. "And he didn't go out of control during the fight. Not only that, he was mindful enough to pull Hana from the situation. That has to mean something."

"He also gave Hana the healing potion," Mason pointed out. "He might be far more intelligent than we thought."

Hana beamed happily. "Of course he is, but he doesn't seem to understand what I'm saying."

"*Rwyf wrth fy modd â Chaerdydd yn y gwanwyn,*" Drysi commented.

Everyone turned to stare are her. Alison wasn't sure if that was Welsh or an incantation.

"I love Cardiff in the spring," the witch explained with a shrug.

"Okay," Alison replied. "I'm sure it's nice. And that's relevant, how?"

"Omni might be intelligent, but he also might not understand most of what anyone is saying. That's all I'm getting at. We don't know where he's from or what he is, and even translation magic relies on a common reference of experience to work properly."

"But he knew enough to give her the potion," Mason observed. "That has to mean something."

"I wouldn't rely on my magic pet to do my healing," Drysi commented. "But at least we know he'll probably do it for Hana."

"For now, we'll keep him at Brownstone Security until we know the situation is more stable," Alison stated. "Tahir, you keep pushing any way you know how. I'll meet Latherby and have him shake the bushes and see what falls out." She turned to Ava. "For now, I don't want any jobs for the primary team. We need to concentrate on this."

The administrative assistant gave a shallow nod. "Of course, Miss Brownstone."

CHAPTER TWENTY

Alison looked around the empty parking lot as she stepped away from her Spider. The wind blew an empty paper bag across the all but deserted space. She layered a shield over herself as she marched toward a black sedan parked in the corner. While she didn't expect any trouble, that didn't mean it might not come.

She arrived at the passenger side and magic radiated off the door. With a sigh, she ran her finger along it and funneled magic into a specific glyph she'd been told to use.

This is overkill. Is he only doing this to fuck with me?

The glyph glowed, and the door clicked. She opened it and slipped inside to settle comfortably in the leather-upholstered seat. Agent Latherby sat in the driver's seat, a concerned look on his face and his hands on the wheel.

"Was all this cloak and dagger really necessary?" she asked. "We've talked about all kinds of secret crap in your office, and now suddenly, we meet in mysterious parking lots with code-glyphs and who knows what else. It's weird."

Her stomach tightened. She hadn't considered the obvious possibility that the PDA agent had stumbled onto something dangerous enough to warrant additional protections.

I hope this isn't the government. I don't have time to deal with a rogue faction. It might have worked out for Dad, but that was only because another group in the government had already targeted them. It's also not like the old days. They hire magicals now.

He shrugged. "I'm only doing what you requested."

Alison frowned. "What are you talking about?"

The agent looked sharply at her, his expression one of slight surprise. "You asked me to be—in your own words —'extremely and unusually circumspect' about this matter, and so I'm being circumspect in an accordingly extreme and unusual way. In addition to the meeting locations and the spells on the doors, I've warded our position and took alternate routes and a number of other measures to minimize the chance that someone might be aware of this particular meeting, Miss Brownstone. That might have been unnecessary, but I do feel I owe you some consideration given the many times you have aided me."

"Fair enough." She chuckled nervously. "I won't be a bitch about you doing exactly what I asked you to do. So what do you have for me? Is it that bad?"

"As the absence of particular evidence is not full proof, I can't fully state that it's either good or bad." He paused for a moment, his expression somber. "I've asked around— discreetly—about any potential governmental ops that might involve you or your people directly or indirectly, whether intended to be hostile or not. I'm not talking about major official operations, either. I can't find even the slightest hint—including pulling strings with certain people who owe me favors—that any government agency is currently targeting you or your people." He frowned intently. "Again, I can't state that this proves there's no one targeting you, but I dug deeply on this, and the available evidence is at least strongly against it."

She absorbed his words, processed the information, and compared it to what she already knew. "I honestly don't know if I'm happy or sad to hear that. This might have been easier if it was simply some group of rogue federal agents trying to pick a fight with me. At the same time, though, I have more of a chance if I'm not dealing with the government."

"I should note," Agent Latherby continued, "that even if the government was involved, it'd make sense for the PDA to be included on some level. We're the agency with the greatest training and experience in dealing with dangerous magical threats. There have been times where we've been used in that capacity, even if we weren't completely aware of all the details." He gave her a measured look. "I do appreciate that you might not feel comfortable enough to share all the information of what might have occurred with me, but I would ask, Miss Brownstone, that if there's something dangerous—a threat to the city—that you inform me. I know you have your reasons to distrust both the government and the PDA in particular, but I think I've long since proven that I'm at least trustworthy."

Alison glanced hastily out the window at some movement. It was only the paper bag from before.

"I'm here right now talking to you because I trust you."

She shook her head. "If I have any reason to believe the situation might change, I'll inform you immediately. But right now, there's no threat to anyone but my people."

Well, my people and our pets.

I've handicapped him by not telling him the truth about Omni, but the more people who know about this, the more danger everyone involved is in, and I don't believe he's a threat to the city. I don't need to put him in an awkward situation where he thinks he needs to contain Omni when the real problem is these suited freaks.

The man nodded slowly and looked forward out the windscreen. There was nothing in front of them but a rusty fence and an empty lot. "With all that said, I did find both NSA- and CIA-sourced warnings that attempted to raise awareness of increased hostile intelligence collection activity in the greater Seattle area. It's spiked particularly in the last six months."

She frowned. "What? You're saying this is the Russians then? Chinese? Oricerans?" She shook her head. "Whoever we were dealing with didn't strike me as Russian or Chinese spies, that's for certain." She shrugged. "Not that I'm an expert on either of those. I'm used to dealing with criminals, not spies."

"Not Russian or Chinese?" His gaze slid back to hold hers. "What about Oriceran?"

"Well...maybe." Alison shrugged. "But they had thousands of years to learn how to spy on humans, and so I think they'd be a little less obvious than the guys I dealt with."

"Fair enough but be aware of the possibility. Something serious may be going on, and if you have reason to believe it involves foreign threats, you need to keep me informed. I appreciate that you have your personal issues and you don't want to drag other people into them, but at the same time, the nature of the threats you face often end up becoming a problem for others."

She nodded. "Will do."

Her thoughts were laden with concerns over the attacks when Alison pulled out of the parking lot in her Fiat. Giving Omni up would have been the easiest solution, but in addition to alienating Hana, that meant turning over a dangerous and mysterious creature to the strange men. She found it hard to believe that anyone who ate strange crystals to mutate themselves had only the safety of the country or planet in mind.

It's almost like Ultimate.

She considered that. There might be a connection there, but at the same time, there could be a connection to a variety of dangerous organizations and powers she'd faced in the past. Ultimate started in Texas, and Hana had found Omni in Seattle, not Texas.

It must be a coincidence, and from what I've heard, Ultimate mutations aren't always the same thing. This is less like Ultimate and more like a potion or a normal artifact.

I have to remember what everyone keeps telling me. I can't personally solve every problem in the country or the city. For now, I need to focus on whoever these men are. Maybe they thought they were doing the right thing. Maybe they didn't, but they almost killed Hana, and there are some things I can't forgive.

Alison's hands tightened around the wheel, and she took a few deep breaths to calm herself. Her friend was okay, and now, it was time to take the fight to those who had ambushed them.

I don't need a truth spell to know those men don't care about Omni because they're worried about him hurting someone. Maybe this ends with us talking it out, but I really doubt that. Some people only understand force, not reason.

———

She was halfway back to her house in her Fiat when the phone rang with a call from Tahir. Automatically, she sent it to speaker and shook her head a few times to try to clear it of some of her lingering dark thoughts. It was time to be a leader. Tahir might not show it in an obvious way, but he loved Hana, and her near death had to eat at him as much as it did at her.

"The meeting with Latherby was a bust," she explained.

"He had no information for you at all?"

"I can't say it was a waste of time," she replied. "He provided decent confirmation that these guys probably aren't anyone in our government, but he also suggested it could be someone in a foreign government."

"That's unlikely."

"I agree."

"Fortunately, I have succeeded where he had failed," the infomancer advised her, his voice infused with smugness.

It was almost comforting to hear him sound like that given the situation.

We're all best when we're acting and thinking like we normally do. If we can defeat the Seventh Order, we can stop these freaks from messing with us.

"You succeeded?" She performed a mirror check, focused more on suspicious cars than normal traffic. She didn't want the suit brigade to damage her beloved vehicle, and that required more situational awareness. "Then give me good news I can really use."

"Yes, I've succeeded in a spectacular manner," he explained. "I just finished my confirmation of the information. At the same time, I won't deny that some of my recent success can be attributed to fortune. I've spent considerable time attempting to trace the earlier message by relying heavily on infomancer techniques, but things keep dead-ending. What I realized is that this failure likely has less to do with superior infomancy on the part of our enemies as opposed to whatever inherent anti-tracking magic our current foes may possess."

"Okay, that makes sense, but how does that help us?" Alison asked.

"Changing my paradigm has allowed me to approach this investigation in a different manner. My earlier confirmation of the fact it was a fake account was based heavily on non-infomancer work. I've focused more on that, as I now realize I will not be able to simply apply superior technique or brute magical force to defeat their defenses. I won't tire you with the entire chain of evidence and techniques, but the important summary point is that I have a possible location to investigate. Unfortunately, my direct drone and cameras efforts fail for no apparent reason, which only raises my suspicion that this location must be associated with our newfound Omni-hunting foes."

She drew a deep breath. "This is good news. And if we pay them a visit on their home turf, they might not have anywhere to easily escape to. We can either finish them off or convince them to stop targeting us or Omni."

"Yes, I'd thought that as well. I'll leave the tactical planning to you, but I'll admit I have a personal interest in seeing them suffer for what they've done."

She grimaced. "There's one small problem with this plan."

"Which is what?" he asked and sounded a little skeptical. She hadn't meant to challenge the genius of his abilities or his accomplishment.

"If we raid what we think is their base, we'll need the whole main team for safety." She rested a single hand on the wheel and gestured with the other, even though he wasn't in the car. "Which means we'll leave Brownstone Security underdefended. These men knew enough to send three separates teams to us on the same night, which means they're probably watching us. If we all show up at their doorstep, they might have a reserve squad ready to raid the building. While I'm confident that Brownstone Security can defend itself when there is at least one of us there, I'm not so sure there won't be casualties without one of us there to counter their abilities. And we don't know if we've seen everything they can do."

"Ah, I understand." He snorted. "But the solution is obvious, don't you think?"

"Um, no, not so obvious." Alison sighed. "I simply don't

want to create trouble for Jerry and the others. They don't even know what's going on with Omni. I don't like keeping all this from them, but there are some secrets that have to remain with us. At the same time, I don't want anyone getting hurt for a secret they aren't a party to."

"Then bring Omni with us. If we can't collectively protect him when we're gathered and have the initiative, it's only a matter of time anyway before they take him, and we might even be fortunate. If he transforms again, he might eliminate many of the enemy himself. He's obviously meant—at least partially—for battle situations."

She considered that for a moment as she changed lanes. "I'll have to think about it, but no matter what, we'll strike and soon.

CHAPTER TWENTY-ONE

The weather might be chilly, but the sun sat high in a sky otherwise unmarred by clouds. It was a pleasant wintery day for a base invasion against a mysterious enemy who might or might not be from Earth or Oriceran.

It's not crazy to think they might be aliens. It can't be impossible for an alien to develop magic, right? They have all kinds of cutting-edge science. Maybe they've done genetic experiments with magical DNA.

Then again, I've based this theory heavily off Hana making one particular comparison. There are thousands of intelligent species on Oriceran, and I don't know probably one-tenth of them. Dad has dealt with Oricerans pretending to be something else more than a few times in his bounty-hunting career.

Or are these guys merely weird humans doing magical experiments on themselves?

Alison sighed at the many possibilities. Where did Omni fit in? If it was only about killing him, it would make more sense for them to approach the government directly and convince them to either send an official team or place a bounty on him. Her father had earned more than a few dollars killing magical creatures at the height of his career.

No. The initial evidence suggested they wanted to capture him, not kill him, which undermined the idea they were concerned with saving people in favor of something else.

Power? Control? Revenge? Who the hell knows? Maybe I can get them to admit something before we have to kill them.

She glanced into the back seat of the SUV. Hana's skin already glowed red from her artifact ring. Her *tachi* sword belt lay at her feet. Omni sat beside her in dog form and panted, his tail wagging, excited for their outing.

This time, they were armed, ready, and knew exactly who they were facing. Tahir's lead directed them to a warehouse in the docks. Cameras near the building constantly failed whenever he aimed them at it, and he'd already lost connection twice with the drone he guided over it when he flew too close, only to regain control after it moved a few hundred feet away.

The SUV was about five minutes away. Whatever tricks their enemies could play with cameras and drones didn't extend to people looking at them. Perhaps that's why they tried to look so similar. She would have a hard time identifying the man who spoke to her out of a line-up of unassuming brown-haired men.

The infomancer kept his drone circling the area and outside the interference zone, but he depended on her to contact him if she thought they needed additional help. Everyone expected to lose contact once they were closer to the warehouse, and they weren't sure if smoke, explosions, or the like would be visible outside the area.

She frowned and glanced at Mason, who was driving. "I just thought of something."

"What?" he asked, still focused on the road ahead of him.

"The fact that both Omni and these guys have anti-tracking abilities suggests there has to be some kind of link. Maybe they're similar species, assuming they're not actually human."

"It's possible," he replied. "I'd say get a sample and test it, but after what you saw at the park, that doesn't seem like a good plan."

"We could simply blow the whole bloody thing up," Drysi suggested with a shrug. "We stand off in the distance, charge up a big spell, and boom. If they're inside that building, we simply have to bring the whole thing down."

Although the Welsh witch had integrated into the team well, every once in a while, she offered a suggestion that reminded her boss that her previous employers were far more ruthless. It wasn't as if Alison could complain too much. Bringing an entire building down had been a featured part of several of her father's plans.

She shook her head. "We can't take the chance of collateral damage, and I'm still willing to give them a chance. If they agree to leave us alone, maybe this doesn't have to be a bloodbath. And talking is the best way to get at least some information from them. They might not be the only ones. We shouldn't have to watch our backs for years."

Hana snorted. "I don't care about giving them another chance. I owe these assholes." She scratched behind Omni's ears, her features set in a scowl.

Alison understood the sentiment. In truth, she was far

more interested in learning about potential future threats than giving the men a pass, but she also understood that at least some focus on personal restraint was for the best.

Drysi nodded at the dog. "And do you really think bringing him is a good idea? It's bringing the hen right to the fox."

"I don't want to go back and find out Brownstone Security was attacked," Alison responded. "This way, we don't have to worry, and it's a warehouse. I'm sure he can find somewhere to hide and change into his Angry Omni mode."

"They likely know you're coming," Tahir warned through their receivers. "Even if they haven't tried to shoot my drone out the air. I did make two passes directly through their field, whatever it is. I could set up a distraction to help."

"No distractions," she replied. "I'm tired of sneaking around. Sometimes, you simply want to get shit done in a simple way. We'll go up there and knock and make some demands. They can either listen, or they can get blasted through a wall."

Mason opened his mouth but shut it when she glared at him.

"Yeah, I know. I sound like Dad. Get over it."

He grinned. "It's not a bad thing. Remember? We're friends now."

Mason steered the SUV toward the side of the warehouse. To their surprise, the building wasn't run down and the power wasn't off. It looked like any other warehouse on the docks, except for a conspicuous lack of workers in the area.

Safety-hatted dock employees in bright orange vests dotted the docks in every direction, along with men and women in other uniforms, but none were closer than a hundred yards to the location.

The team had lost contact with Tahir about thirty seconds before and Alison had been surprised by the relatively low levels of magic she felt. That kind of extended ward would normally give off a strong magical signature. It again made her question who they would actually face.

Low-level repulsion ward? Only enough to keep them hidden without being too noticeable, maybe?

There's still so much we don't understand about what's going on and who we're dealing with. That's one big reason right there not to blow the building up. And I don't think the cops and PDA would appreciate it if I start resolving all my problems with high levels of massive property destruction, even though half the time, they act like I'm already doing that.

Don't they get it? I'm the neutron bomb of Brownstones. I eliminate the people and leave the building intact.

The SUV rolled to a stop, and Mason put on the parking brake as surprise inched onto his face.

"They haven't tried to blow us up yet," he commented. "That's promising." He retrieved his wand from his jacket holster to cast his shield and enhancement spells. "But I doubt this will end with us agreeing to disagree and go on our merry way, A."

"I do, too. But who knows? Maybe we'll get lucky." She

snorted. "According to my dad, Brownstone's aren't that lucky."

"You found me, didn't you?" He grinned.

Drysi cracked her knuckles and fluffed the lapels of the long black duster she currently wore. She'd crammed two dozen enchanted daggers into sheaths inside, in addition to sporting a holster for her 9mm and her wand. "I still think we should look away and let Omni do his thing. He's already proven he can annihilate these bastards."

Hana ruffled the animal's fur. "I don't think it really works that way. I thought about that. When he's in his normal forms, he acts like those forms. Maybe a smart version, but I think something about being in battle mode made him closer to being like us. I also…kind of already tried that experiment."

Alison blinked. "What?"

"This morning. I left him alone after telling him to turn into Angry Omni." She shrugged. "When I came back, he was a cockatiel."

Mason snickered. "My brother has a cockatiel. Many of them are fairly angry."

Alison layered a few shields over herself, alternating between light and shadow magic this time. She opened the door and shook her head. "This might have started because of Omni, but my gut says there's a lot more here than one strange shape-changing pet. If we go in there and talk, maybe we can learn some of that."

"And if they attack us first?" Drysi asked, an eyebrow raised.

"Then we repay their courtesy." She frowned and stepped outside. "I'm not here to get punched in the nose.

I'm here to make sure no one wakes Tahir and Hana in the middle of the night."

A loud grinding noise echoed among the nearby buildings. The loading bay door about thirty yards away started opening.

"Oh, that's convenient." She shrugged.

"I did want to at least blow the door in," the witch muttered with a shrug. "What's the bloody point of even bringing so many explosive daggers if I don't get to use them?"

Alison extended a shadow blade and shook her head. "These guy's little trick with disrupting communications and tracking might mean we don't have to worry about AET showing up to spoil the fun. You might still have any number of chances to blow things up."

Hana stepped out of the SUV and strapped her sword belt on. She foxed out immediately and grinned. "Oh, last time, I bet they felt good about kicking my ass. I can't wait to show them how tough a fully equipped Hot Fox is."

"Remember, we need information first if possible," her boss reminded her. She marched toward the almost open loading bay door. "Because whoever these guys are, I doubt this one building is their entire organization. I don't want to spend the next year dealing with them in groups of a half-dozen like we had to do with the Seventh Order."

Omni hopped out of the SUV and padded after Hana. His tail wagged happily as if they were on a merry walk through the park. He didn't seem to care about the chilly temperatures or the harsh winds that blew off the bay. Maybe he was thinking of all the people he wanted to kill.

Hana was fighting those men, and he probably got away

early on, but he didn't transform. He didn't bother to until it looked like she was in trouble, and I doubt he'll do it again. Maybe it was a mistake to bring him, but the only way to knock the truth loose is to dangle the bait.

The four magicals and their dog marched toward the open warehouse like they were auditioning for their own hyperviolent version of the *Wizard of the Oz*. As the Brownstone team closed to within ten yards, the almost identical brown-haired men in dark suits boiled out of the back rooms to fill the main bay. None of them held guns, and they all lacked the darkened veins and black eyes Hana had described.

They aren't immediately itching for a fight, but they do want to make a show of a force. I can work with that.

Alison slowed her pace and stepped into the warehouse. The others entered after her and surveyed the area warily.

Dozens of men stood in the warehouse and all watched the new arrivals with neutral expressions betraying nothing about what they felt. They didn't look happy, sad, afraid, or excited. Their arms hung at their sides, and none crouched or stood in a defensive stance. They stood so rigidly they could have been mistaken for statues.

She pointed to the loading bay door. "You might as well close it. If this ends up getting violent, there's less chance that innocent people will be hurt. Before, you acted like you cared on some small level about not hurting people. So prove it to me, and maybe this doesn't have to end badly."

Here goes the first test.

The loading bay door began to descend loudly.

Mason laughed. "A, you just cut off our line of retreat."

She narrowed her eyes. "Whatever happens in the next

few minutes, we won't retreat. We'll come to some sort of agreement, or we'll make it so they're afraid to step in the same time zone as us."

The fox patted her hilt. "I can hardly wait."

Omni's tail stopped wagging. He paced behind Hana and growled quietly.

Now that they were inside, Alison could feel more magic from all around her. It seemed to radiate from every single man in the room, but there were no obvious shields or wands. Whoever and whatever these men were, they weren't wizards.

Maybe Agent Latherby was onto something. They might be some weird Oriceran group pretending to be human. That might explain why they all look so similar.

Drysi coughed. "What do we do now?"

The team all looked at Alison for direction.

"They haven't attacked us immediately," she commented. "That's a good sign." She turned to the assembled army. "I'm Alison Brownstone, CEO of Brownstone Security. Some in this city call me the Dark Princess."

It's a long shot, but this could be some sort of messed-up Drow princess test. I might as well throw all the bait out at once.

After a moment of consideration, she added, "I am also the Drow Princess of the Shadow Forged, but I don't represent the Drow people. I come here today in defense of my friends and employees, and…uh, a pet, Omni."

That sounded far more impressive in my head.

Drysi snickered but stopped when Hana glared at her.

Alison raised her shadow blade. The men needed to understand that she was serious. She wasn't there as a supplicant. She was there to make demands.

"You have claimed that this is all about Omni being dangerous," she shouted. "But you also made it clear you were willing to hurt Hana to recover him. The only time he's been dangerous is when he killed your men after they attempted to kill her. The whole point of Brownstone Security is to protect innocent people. If you can provide evidence that you actually give a crap about protecting this city, we can discuss Omni." She gestured to the dog, who now sat on his haunches beside Hana. "Otherwise, this will end with many dead people, and this time, you're not surprising an unarmed woman walking her dog."

The crowd remained silent. They watched the team and only occasionally blinked but barely moved otherwise.

"This is one of the creepiest situations I've ever been in," Drysi muttered, "and I used to work for a megalomaniac dark wizard."

Mason frowned. "I don't think it's working, A."

"They aren't attacking, are they?" she replied and took a deep breath. "In the parking garage, one of your men talked about taking orders. He refused to tell us who gave the orders, but I want to talk to that person now. I need to understand who you are and why you're doing this. I don't think that's unreasonable, and let me make myself clear. I'm prepared to destroy you today if I think you're a threat to my people."

The thick silence stretched for several interminable seconds before the crowd parted to allow a single figure to walk through. He was yet another nondescript brown-haired man. His suit wasn't distinct or special and his tie was the same solid color design as every one of his comrades.

"I'm beginning to wonder how they tell each other apart," Alison murmured.

"Maybe they smell different." Hana sniffed the air.

"Or they see in a different spectrum," Mason suggested.

The man strolled forward with no evidence of haste in his pace nor any hint of concern in his expression. He stopped in front of the crowd of men and tilted his head to stare at Alison.

"You are Alison Brownstone," he declared.

"I am. Who are you? And don't you dare tell me I don't need to know. I'm through with games."

He straightened his head and blinked once. "Whether you need to know remains undetermined, but our estimates suggest this encounter can possibly be resolved without a significant loss of resources by providing you with minimum information to sate your curiosity."

She scoffed. "Yeah, I guess you could say that. You seem to know a lot about us, but we don't know anything about you, so let's start with who you are."

"I am the Weaver for these Strands. In a sense, you could say I lead them, even if I myself am led by another. We are the Tapestry."

CHAPTER TWENTY-TWO

Strands? That's what they call these guys? I guess Boring Bills doesn't sound as cool.

Alison glanced at her friends. They all shrugged to indicate that they didn't know the group. She hadn't heard of the name or any organization that remotely resembled the men they were dealing with, so she hadn't done much to narrow the range of possibilities even to a planet of origin.

"Okay, Weaver," She replied. "What's your deal?"

The Weaver pointed at Omni. "You've brought it here. That's useful. It shows that on some level, you understand that you don't have to be our enemies. Now, you will hand it over. If you do so, there need be no immediate enmity between us despite the fact that you have killed Strands."

"Your Strands died because they attacked Hana." She shook her head. "Not good enough. See, you need to understand. This isn't me surrendering to you. I'm not here to beg for your forgiveness. This is me giving you one last chance to convince me why you're not my enemies and why I shouldn't annihilate you down to the last Strand."

She pointed at Hana. "You almost killed her. The only reason she didn't die was because she had a healing potion on her. If she had died, this would be a very different conversation."

"Hana Sugimoto resisted the Strands," the Weaver replied. He continued to speak in the same flat voice they had heard from the others during their previous encounters. "She was given her opportunity to surrender the creature, and she violently refused. Her injuries are the natural result of her actions."

"The way I heard it, you showed up with lies and threats, including suggesting you would take an innocent hostage to force her to do what you wanted." Alison glared at the man, if that was what he was. "And don't try to feed me a line about how you're all government agents. I don't know who or what you are, but you're definitely not government agents."

He nodded. "We are not agents of the American government. That is accurate."

"Russian? Chinese?" It was worth a shot.

"We are not agents of the Russian or Chinese governments."

Alison narrowed her eyes. "Are you Oriceran?"

The man tilted his head. "Your questions are irrelevant to the dispensation of the creature Omni. Hand him over."

"The questions are relevant to me, and I'm the woman commanding a group of powerful magicals who are here and ready to eliminate your Strands." She pointed her sword at him. "I didn't fight you, but Hana did. I know your kind can die."

"Fear of death doesn't frighten us," the Weaver replied.

"Such feeble attempts to manipulate us indicate that you have a weak understanding of the Tapestry."

"Of course I do. That's why I'm asking these questions."

Her adversary stared at Omni. "Your reluctance to comply with our request is puzzling given the available information you have on the situation. The creature Omni is very dangerous. You must know that now since it showed its true form and what it is capable of. It is a killer, a remorseless animal that thirsts for blood. The forms it takes are a deception, nothing more."

Yeah, I bet you know a thing or two about deception.

Hana scoffed. "Yeah, he's so thirsty for blood that he's never hurt anyone the entire time I owned him until you assholes nearly killed me. That totally sounds like a rabid monster."

Alison nodded. "Let's set that aside. Say he's exactly what you claim, a deadly animal. Are you saying the Tapestry is some kind of magical animal control agency? I've never heard of you before."

The Weaver shook his head. "That's not accurate over-all, but it is accurate enough in this particular scenario. Whatever you believe you understand about that creature is but a small fraction of what you don't know. Your ignorance means you cannot generate plans based on accurate estimates of probabilities."

"I don't know him?" She snorted. "I could say the same thing about you. Here's the thing, Weaver. I work closely with the PDA in Seattle, and if there was some truly out of control magical creature, they would be the people at the top of the list to handle it, not you and your bland suit brigade who run around lying about who you are."

"Our estimates suggested you might have this reaction. The probability of you being reasonable was non-zero. Sometimes, our estimates are off."

Drysi snickered. "He has a right mouth, doesn't he?"

Mason nodded with a frown.

Alison narrowed her eyes. "Give me a reason to even consider handing Omni over to you. A real reason based on real information, not the crap you keep telling me about how deadly and out of control he is. You claim we don't know enough about him, so explain what we're supposed to know."

The man's face twitched, the closest thing she had seen to emotion on it yet. "The creature was being transported when an accident occurred. It escaped. In the process of its escape, people died. More will die if you don't hand him over."

"What people? Your people? That's not enough information." She pointed to the loading bay door. "Because I know the AET, local bounty hunters, PDA, and FBI weren't talking about some crazed magical monster killing people around the time Hana found him. That kind of thing would have been all over the news."

"Hana Sugimoto's previous encounter was against a smaller force of Strands." The Weaver pointed behind him. "We are aware of your personal power, but our estimates suggest that we have sufficient forces to defeat you if necessary."

Alison laughed. "Wow. Right back to the threats, and I assume that in your weird little head, it's actually supposed to be intimidating. Mostly, it simply pisses me off."

"It is merely a statement of the estimated probabilities.

Are you so sure you can engage us in battle and not suffer losses? Are you willing to do it for a dangerous creature you have no reason to protect?"

Hana gripped the hilt of her sword. Drysi's hand drifted toward the inside of her jacket. Mason took a few steps to the side.

Alison raised her shadow blade in front of her face. "That's what you don't seem to understand. You insist that Omni's dangerous and your only proof is that he kicked your asses when you attacked Hana. I've been on the fence about the whole thing but now, I'm not convinced he's dangerous. I'm convinced that you guys need him for something I'm likely to be pissed about. Something I should probably stop right now."

The Weaver shook his head. "Your motivations do not change our probability estimates."

"What about my people?" She channeled energy to her legs. "Your men lost to only Hana and Omni, and now, she has three friends with her."

"Oh." The Weaver nodded. "I understand. Your personal probability estimates have been made without knowledge of our full capabilities. Additional measures have been authorized." He reached into his jacket and withdrew a thin black rod.

She pointed her blades. "What's that?"

"I am not lying when I state this will not harm you." He raised the rod.

Her stomach clenched as waves of magic passed over her. The walls began to glow. Omni howled in pain and fell onto his side.

Hana's eyes widened and her tails went rigid. She stared at the writhing animal. "What are you doing to him?"

"Neutralizing his capability for the moment," the Weaver replied. "The pain is temporary. We detected your drone earlier, so we summoned all our remaining forces to overwhelm you if necessary."

Omni whimpered and fell unconscious.

"What is the Tapestry?" Alison demanded. "You're with the Alliance, aren't you? You're testing magic on Earth now? Is that what this is?"

"Who the hell are the Alliance?" Hana asked. She yanked her blade out of her sheath and glared at the man.

Every single Strand in the room retrieved a spiked crystal from his jacket except their leader. This time, however, the crystals were different colors—black, white, red, and blue, among others.

"Are you speaking of the Nine Systems Alliance?" he asked and shook his head. "We are aware of this organization, but we don't understand what it is. It has eluded our investigation except for the name and a connection to an incident in LA, but that doesn't matter for now. It is clear you will refuse to cooperate, and you already know too much information. Your continued existence presents a threat to our estimates if you're unwilling to cooperate. We appreciate that you're powerful, but you will not be able to win against so many Strands consuming True Cores."

"Is that what they're called?" Alison muttered. She'd never heard the term applied to artifacts before, consumable or otherwise.

The army of Strands swallowed their crystals. Their

veins darkened and their eyes turned solid black. Muted ripples of magic filled the room.

"You didn't transform, Weaver." She pointed one of her blades at him. "If a fight starts, you'll die first."

"That's an accurate estimate, but it is irrelevant to whether or not you'll survive." He pointed at her. "Kill the Dark Princess first to maximize the probability of victory."

Every Strand in the room turned to face her.

And now, we end the diplomatic portion of our program and go straight to the ass-kicking portion.

CHAPTER TWENTY-THREE

Let's get this done. I gave them their chance.

L Alison released the energy in her legs. She flew into the army of Strands and bypassed the Weaver. He had chosen not to strengthen himself for the fight, which meant he wasn't an immediate threat. Not only that, if he didn't want to fight, he would be useful for interrogation. There was still far more she needed to learn about the Tapestry.

The momentum carried her forward and powered her blade to pierce a Strand's chest and emerge on the other side. He fell, his eyes open in a death stare. She yanked the blade out and summoned another in her other hand.

Okay, there is an army of these guys, but at least they aren't that hard to eliminate.

With a grin, Drysi tossed a dagger into the far flank of the enemy line. The explosion scattered several of the enemy, but one remained untouched and his skin glowed yellow for a moment.

Okay, some are harder than others to kill, but that's not a big deal.

Alison stabbed the two on either side of her as they turned to attack her. Several more spun and raised their fists, their black eyes impossible to read.

Hana and Mason barreled into the fight on opposite sides of Alison. The fox slashed with her blade. The *tachi* had no difficulty in cutting into the hardened flesh of the enhanced Strands. Three swings eliminated three enemies. She dodged a blow before she thrust her blade through an attacker's heart.

Mason pounded a fist into one man's head with a resounding thud. The Strand hurtled back and collided with one of his comrades. They fell together and tripped a few others.

We can do this. There's a lot of them, but we've fought tougher enemies.

Alison stabbed and cut with her shadow blades. A couple of their adversaries absorbed a few more strikes and their skin glowed yellow. She turned and one struck her with a red glowing fist. She careened back with a grunt of pain when her shields soaked up only part of the blow. Impact with another enemy ended her unplanned flight. She ran him through with both blades before she thrust onto her feet and cut another Strand in half.

These guys hit damned hard. I'm surprised Hana did as well as she did without any shields the first time she fought them.

Several attackers surrounded Mason and pummeled him with their own enhanced blows. He stumbled and his shields strained as he returned the punches and managed to knock a few of his opponents down. His powerful uppercut crunched into the jaw of a glowing yellow Strand. The man spun a few times before he collapsed. The wizard's spin-kick launched another of his assailants into a nearby pack and disrupted their attempts to surround him. Tension lined his features. He didn't look afraid, but he didn't seem to enjoy himself as much as Drysi had earlier.

The Welsh witch darted constantly from one side to the other as her arm whipped explosive daggers into concentrations of Strands and scattered them. Her earlier glee was replaced by an expression of grim resignation as she attempted to thin the massive army to a more manageable number. Some of the men rose again, charred but moving, while others remained on the ground. The acrid smell of their burns mingled in the air.

Whatever the Strands were and whatever consuming the crystals did, they were still living beings. Defeating them was a matter of applying enough force to deliver a fatal wound. Their main current advantage was sheer numbers.

They had enough to send three different teams after us, plus more in reserve. But the Weaver said he brought everyone in to kick our asses. If we finish them here, that'll be enough for a while, at least.

Alison carved through foe after foe until she finally stood back-to-back with Hana.

"These guys are really annoying," the fox shouted as she slashed the throat of an attacker.

"Sure," she replied. "They aren't my favorite people in the world right now." A man tried to flank and she stabbed him in the stomach.

The Drow princess and the sword-wielding fox hurtled

in opposite directions and launched into a series of quick slashes that parted the wall of Strands that surrounded them. Several of the yellow-shielded men converged on Hana, only to find her *tachi* made short work of their defenses with only a few blows.

Many victims of the *tachi* had made that mistake when they assumed it was merely a sword, rather than a unique blade with a powerful enchantment. Even James Brownstone had underestimated it years before. Better wielded, the sword might have ended his life before he adapted fully to its magic.

The fox grinned. "That's what you get for messing me and my pet, assholes. I owe you for that beating."

Her flurry of movement ended with another fatality among the enemy ranks, but she frowned as a green glow suffused a couple of bodies near her. Their wounds closed, and they stood to face her.

"Seriously? Now you're really getting on my nerves."

She impaled one through the heart and quickly yanked her blade free. The wounded man fell, still bathed in the light green glow. She growled and decapitated another regenerating Strand. This time, he didn't resurrect.

An assailant tackled her and as they sprawled together, her sword slid out of her reach. His fists were like pistols as he pounded her head. Her shield dimmed noticeably, but she clawed his throat out before she rolled over to retrieve her blade and scrambled to her feet to meet several more who swarmed toward her.

Alison hacked through another group before she vaulted upward and extended her wings. She released her swords and rocketed toward the roof, out of the reach of the hard, bone-shattering blows of the Strands. She'd had to constantly feed energy into her shields to keep them from collapsing. It was easy to believe that without them, each punch would be like being hit by a truck.

Damn. If I didn't have the others with me, these bastards might have been able to overwhelm me. I guess the Weaver wasn't totally full of shit. This is a halfway decent fight, but I need to reset the tactical tempo before everyone gets too exhausted. The Strands die easily enough, but they don't seem to show much in the way of pain or exertion.

Mason staggered back from a trio of Strands who each landed quick jabs. She tossed three shadow crescents. The powerful missiles drove through the attackers, and they fell almost as one. Now, with more room to maneuver, the life wizard rallied and clotheslined another charging adversary, whose head cracked painfully on the concrete when he fell. Alison spent the next ten or so seconds laying down cover fire from above.

With the Strands no longer clumped into easy collective targets, Drysi gave up on her explosive daggers and changed to her wand. She obliterated one man with a white-hot fireball from only a few yards away. A few of the others attempted to attack her, but she yanked her pistol out and put a bullet into each of their heads. When one began to glow green, she emptied her clip into his head until he stopped moving.

The entire army was now spread out in distinct clusters around the four Brownstone team members. While they had strength, bravery, and numbers, there was a distinct lack of tactics on display. Most simply waited until there was an opening before they charged forward to punch or kick their victim into submission. Alison was reminded more of an insect swarm attempting to overwhelm an enemy.

You guys should call yourself the Swarm rather than the Tapestry. I wonder if not all of them can talk. Every time, it's been one guy who spoke for them.

She circled the room and continued to pepper the army with light blasts or shadow crescents. Most of her assaults eliminated the enemy with a single strike, but a few of the shielded Strands required two or three direct attacks to defeat them. The numbers were becoming more manageable, but the sweat and grimaces on Drysi and Mason's faces suggested they were under strain.

Everyone's too close together. If I tried a shadow nova, I'd kill my own friends.

Compared to the others, Hana continued to cleave her enemies with ease with the help of the magical penetrating power of the *tachi*. Even in her case, sweat poured down her face, and the red glow around her skin had dimmed from repeated attacks. If her artifact field went down, one solid blow to the head might kill her.

Several Strands surrounded her friend and Alison crippled them with a barrage of shadow crescents.

Based on her aerial view, about half the enemy lay defeated on the ground. Unfortunately, collateral damage risk from area attacks remained, so she continued her rapid strafing runs and shifted between targets around Hana, Mason, and Drysi. Her volleys didn't allow any of the enemy to build up momentum or cluster together, as her team's defenses continued to brush close to their limits and she had the opportunity to spare them a concerted attack.

The Strands' punches must not only be about hitting hard. They must have some kind of low-level anti-magic capability, too. That would explain the Weaver's confidence, but it also means that Angry Omni was able to take these heavy blows without the several layers of shields I use. There has to be more to him. I doubt he could have survived this entire army himself.

Alison finished the thought by thrusting her palms out to launch a bright lance of light magic. The missile careened down and exploded against two of the enemy that attempted to sneak up on Drysi. Their bodies bounced and rolled, and the witch offered her a grin and a thumbs-up.

I need to draw more of them off to give everyone time to process strategy.

She released her wings and summoned a shadow blade with her left arm as she fired rapid staccato blasts into the Strand army.

"I'm now available for a quick dance, assholes!" she shouted.

Several turned to attack her. She felled them with light blasts before she stabbed a couple of others who managed to close the distance and threatened to punch, kick, or tackle her.

With the remainder of the army now split into four groups, they became easy targets for the Brownstone team. Hana uttered a howling war cry as she swung her sword to annihilate enemy after enemy. A stone-faced Mason alternated punches and bullets as he defeated his last few adversaries. A bleeding, limping Drysi advanced with her wand in front of her after she'd cracked the skull of a Strand with her empty pistol.

Alison fired a shadow crescent into one Strand before she sliced him from stomach to neck with her blade. He collapsed, and she paused a moment to drag in several deep breaths. She spun, her gaze searching for more enemies.

Every Strand lay on the blood-painted floor, wounded, dying, or dead. To her surprise, the Weaver lay on the ground, still alive and half-sitting up, his pants charred and his legs badly burned. She had wondered if he would try to run. His presence there earned him a smidgen of respect.

"Good," she announced. "I'm glad to see you're still alive because I have a few more questions." She strode toward the wounded man.

CHAPTER TWENTY-FOUR

Alison hesitated for a moment to scrutinize her team. Drysi was casting a healing spell on her injuries and Mason looked more tired than injured. Despite the sweat soaking her body, Hana's face was a mask of satisfaction.

"I am impressed, Alison Brownstone," the Weaver declared. "You have earned victory where you could easily have earned death."

She pointed her blade at his throat. "You guys are terrible at estimating probabilities. None of this had to happen. None at all."

"Estimates are merely that—estimates of probabilities," he replied, still as monotone as ever despite lying severely wounded in a room with his dead comrades. "Very few probabilities approach one hundred percent, even in maximal circumstances. It's not surprising that on occasion, the less probable event occurs. Such is the nature of probability."

"What is the Tapestry?" she demanded. "That sounds like some weird band name, but I don't understand what you are. Magicals? Non-magicals? And what is Omni really, and what does he have to do with any of this?"

The Weaver shook his head. "There is no longer any utility in me answering your questions. Accordingly, I shall refrain from answering until such time as you offer me an incentive for your cooperation."

"Are you serious?" She glared at him. "I'm the woman with a sword to your throat. My small team obliterated your army."

"Our intelligence suggests that slaughtering a prisoner is outside the typical behavior range you display."

"You're willing to bet your life on more probability estimates?"

He tilted his head to regard her with his habitual blank expression. "My life does not matter. We do not fear death for we are the Tapestry. If you wish to kill me, then kill me. I will not provide you any additional useful information without you providing mutual benefit in exchange. This is not an unreasonable position, even for a prisoner."

Alison took several deep breaths before she released her blade. "You've lost badly. You underestimated my team. I won't say you didn't manage some good strikes, but I didn't lose anyone, and you lost everyone."

"Yes. We didn't anticipate the need for elite forces given the large numbers of Strands available. It will take time for the other Weavers to realize what has happened, but they will learn from our mistake." He stared at her with no hint of the pain he must be feeling on his face. "In the next battle in which you face our forces, you are far more likely, accordingly, to be defeated."

She was about to demand information about the elite

forces but decided against it. He had already made it clear he didn't intend to answer any direct questions, but in his arrogance, he'd already given up useful intelligence.

"And where are the rest of the Tapestry?" Alison asked. "I'd so like to meet them."

"There is no utility in my providing that information, but there is a high probability that you will encounter Strands of the Tapestry again."

"Don't get too excited, if that's even possible." She scoffed. "I won't execute you, but I won't let you go. I'll call the PDA because a dangerous army of magical-crystal-popping thugs seems like the kind of thing they care about." She gestured around the room. "Do you see all this? It's convinced me that this problem isn't only about my team anymore. If you can field this many men with those True Cores, you're more dangerous than the average gang in this city."

"Imprisoning me will gain you nothing."

"Who's in command? Where are they now?" she shouted. Frustration erased her earlier plan to conduct a more subtle interrogation.

"I will force a resolution." He inhaled deeply and leapt at Alison despite his burned legs, his hands outstretched. A shot rang out, and blood splattered from his jerking head. He fell back with a new bullet hole.

Mason stood nearby, his gun pointed and a glare on his face. "Are you okay, A?"

Alison sighed. "You didn't need to do that. I had everything under control."

"Maybe." He frowned. "These guys still have their tricks, A. You can't let your guard down."

"What the hell is happening?" Hana shouted and pointed.

Several of the men sizzled, not only their skin but also their clothes. Their bodies and garments vaporized into a faint black mist that slowly diffused throughout the room. Even a phone on the ground began to dissolve. Again, the level of magic emitted from the effect was noticeably lower than Alison would have expected from the process, but she didn't understand what it all meant.

"This explains where all the bodies went," she muttered and shook her head.

Mason wrinkled his nose, disgust all over his face. "No witnesses, huh? No evidence?"

Drysi looked around the room. Almost all the bodies had begun the disintegration process.

"That's one trick the Seventh Order should have thought of," she commented. "Although compartmentalization serves its purpose without being so dramatic."

Omni shook his head and stood. He barked happily and wagged his tail, the effects of the Tapestry attack now gone. The room with the slowly disappearing slaughtered Strands apparently made his day.

Mason glanced into his rear-view mirror as they pulled away from the warehouse. "Is that it? We're going to leave it there? That was a major base for them."

"It was a glorified hotel room." Alison shrugged. "We already checked the whole place. There was nothing special there. I'll talk to Latherby about the Tapestry to let him know about this warehouse, but I'll keep Omni's existence a little less clear. I'll make up an explanation about them hunting magical animals or something, so he can at least understand our confusion."

After they had finished healing from the battle, the Brownstone team had investigated the warehouse. They had hoped to gain intelligence that would provide details of the mysterious Tapestry.

With the deaths of the Strands and the Weaver, whatever anti-tracking and anti-magic field they had emitted collapsed and allowed Tahir to establish contact. He'd already hacked into several warehouse computers to aid their investigation efforts, and from what he could tell, the devices contained old inventory information from the previous owners but nothing else.

Perhaps the Tapestry men hadn't had time to fully establish themselves, but after everything Alison had seen in the fight, she began to question if the Strands were true individuals.

I suppose it doesn't matter for now. It's more important to keep track of their general capabilities. We know how hard they hit, even when you have magic shields, and how fast they can move. We know some have shields, and some can regenerate. But we don't know why they don't all have those abilities. There's some hidden limitation we haven't seen, a weakness we can use against them.

Omni sat quietly on the seat between Hana and Drysi, still in dog form and his eyes half-closed.

"I'm satisfied with how that went down," Hana declared with a smile. "Very satisfied. I got my revenge on those bastards, and we sent them a lesson about messing with Brownstone Security."

Drysi grinned. "Nothing like a right proper thrashing to get the blood going. I don't know how much real villainy the Tapestry are into, but not everyone has to be the Seventh Order."

Mason frowned. "From what the Weaver said, this isn't over, though. That wasn't all the Tapestry. That wasn't even their best guys. Isn't anyone worried about that?"

Alison shook her head. "It doesn't matter if it's not over forever. It's over for now. He honestly thought he would win with sheer numbers. They might have some special elite forces tucked away in Topeka or something, but after us annihilating an entire warehouse full of them, that'll at least give them some pause. They'll probably spend more time watching us if they haven't been already."

"And Omni?" Mason asked with a quick glance over his shoulder. "He's effectively a living target we've slapped on our backs."

"I still have no idea what he is, but after dealing with them, I know I don't want the Tapestry to have him. With the local forces defeated and all the wards Tahir has on his and Hana's home, I think it'll be fine for Omni to go back there at night, but I'll also change policy. It might be helpful for Omni to be at the building during the day, at least until we've finally eliminated the Tapestry."

He snickered. "You say that so casually."

"There's no reason to shy away from the truth. We'll have to do it eventually."

"Fine, but getting back to the pets. Won't people notice that Hana has a variety of different pets?"

She shrugged. "Everyone already thinks she's quirky."

"I prefer sexy and lovable," Hana interjected.

"People," Alison continued and ignored her friend for the moment, "will merely assume she has a zoo of pets at home, and if Omni turns into something too exotic, she can simply not bring him that day. If other people want to bring pets, it's fine. I'll put some money into a little indoor dog park, maybe a cat room, or something like that. It won't be full-time doggy daycare or anything, but it'll be enough to provide a plausible reason to have him there during the day."

"All that simply to provide cover for Omni?" Mason asked.

"Yeah." She shrugged. "He's still the key to whatever's going on with the Tapestry, and I'd prefer to keep him close and guarded whenever possible. Ava and Sonya already know the truth, and that's fine for now. I'll consider briefing Jerry if he needs to know. I'm not convinced he does yet. Too many secrets are annoying."

Hana patted Omni's head. "Good. The Brownstone Building's a little too sterile for my baby. We need a few improvements to make it worthy of him."

Drysi's smile disappeared. "It got lost in all that blood and guts, but Hana asked the question, and now I'll ask it. What's the Nine Systems Alliance, Alison? I've never heard of them before, but you seemed convinced the Tapestry were part of it."

Mason glanced Alison's way, curiosity on his face. The fox nodded.

"I want to tell you." She sighed. "But I can't tell you yet. I need to get permission from someone first."

"The government?" the life wizard asked.

Alison snorted. "No. I'm sure they wouldn't want me to talk about it, but they're not my concern. I'll check with the people I need to, and I'll get back to you all soon. You're right, you deserve to know the truth."

The witch folded her arms and nodded with a mollified expression. Hana looked more curious than annoyed, as did Mason.

"Thanks for understanding."

CHAPTER TWENTY-FIVE

The Forbidden Bean was always busy, filled with employees from all the nearby businesses, not only Brownstone Security. It also had the advantage of being a place where people were used to seeing Alison. She wasn't a spectacle there, merely another part of the scenery.

She sipped her Frappuccino as she waited in her corner booth. A cup sat across from her. She'd already taken the liberty of ordering for her conversation partner. A few minutes passed before her guest entered the shop and headed toward her.

Rasila settled opposite her, a slight smile on her face. The other Drow princess maintained her disguise of Ruby, a young, dark-haired human woman with a mole on her cheek.

Something about that always vaguely annoyed Alison, but she also didn't want the other woman to be too obvious either and a young Drow woman would definitely be memorable. As much as she would have preferred to not care about any such political concerns, either on Earth or Oriceran, the situation demanded it.

I wonder if the other princesses know about her human identity. Do they pay as much attention to Earth as she does, or are they as clueless about modern Earth culture as Myna was?

Rasila gestured to the cup waiting for her. "We've done this enough that you even know my preferences." She looked around the room, a smirk on her face. "And so quiet. It's very convenient for discussion."

Alison shrugged. "I didn't see a reason to wait for you before casting the spell. I think you have to realize by now I'm not here to play games. You've claimed you want to be my ally, and one way to do that is for us to get to know each other better. That's why I've had coffee and lunch with you more lately."

"It's also so I can provide you with intelligence, yes?" Her companion chuckled quietly. "Let's be clear about that. I don't mind lies to our inferiors, but we princesses should always be honest with each other. It's a matter of respect."

Sure, she says that after tricking me with a fake job so she can test me.

Alison frowned. "I have a busy schedule lately and there is only so much time I can take out of it for a Drow princess who tried to kill me. So, yeah, I need to get a little something out of it."

"The same Drow princess who now wonders if you should be queen." Rasila sighed and looked disappointed. "You're so dreary at times, Alison, which is amusing considering you grew up on Earth rather than Oriceran immersed in Drow politics. You're almost like Miar that way, but she's more trapped by outdated views on what honor is, whereas you can be more direct and understand that too much honor can be a straitjacket." She nodded. "I do appreciate your blunt way of handling certain matters. It's no wonder your influence has grown so quickly in this city. Actually, I suppose that's why I've taken a liking to you, Alison. Besides your raw power, you combine the best traits of the other princesses—the martial valor of Novati, the honor of Miar, and the pragmatism of Drae."

She nodded and simply let the unstated implications hang in the air for a moment. It seemed like she was destined to always have at least one Drow obsessed with pushing her into their politics no matter how loudly she proclaimed her disinterest.

"Speaking of the princesses, are any moving?" she asked. "I would prefer to be prepared if they try something."

Rasila took a sip of her coffee. She set the cup down and inhaled deeply, wafting the fumes toward her with her hand. "I'll give this to humans. They can do some wonderful things with beans, and they manage it without magic. Give them a few more thousand years, and they won't be complete savages." She chuckled. "No. None of the princesses are on the move—not against you or me anyway. Things have been quieter than I anticipated, and I think you're fine for now. In truth, the Guardians are attempting some nonsense with law reform that has gained their focus. We princesses have been so focused on each other and contemptuous of the Guardians, we sometimes forget they are the ones still controlling the Drow and we have to tread carefully."

Alison nodded. "As far as I'm concerned, that's all good.

It means less chance of someone else coming to mess with me when I have a ton of other crap to deal with."

"Indeed. It occurs to me we're meeting regularly now near your seat of power." Her companion studied her casually but a little speculatively. "You know my coffee preferences by memory, and we chat about both personal and professional matters."

"Yeah. So? What are you getting at?" She took another sip of her drink.

"I think, dear Princess of the Shadow Forged, you're at risk of befriending me." Rasila chuckled. "Despite the initial derision and scorn you felt toward me."

She shrugged. "You're not so bad when you're not obsessing over fighting me or putting me on the throne."

"Oh, I still obsess over both. I've merely found it's better to be less vocal about it. But if you don't want to consider us friends, at least consider us allies. I know you have strong feelings about not wanting to be involved in Drow politics, but it doesn't hurt to maintain some contacts, right?"

"Allies?" Alison frowned. "I don't know if I'd go that far, but I'll say for now we're not enemies, and we can work toward being allies and maybe eventually, friends."

"Wonderful," Rasila responded. "Whether you seek the throne or not, you'll be a woman of influence and power on this planet and Oriceran. Gather all the allies you can, Alison. You never know when you'll need them."

"Don't I know it," she grumbled.

Alison yawned as she put up the footrest on her recliner in the living room. Mason and Sonya had already gone to bed. She should have been in bed, too, but she'd been restless and didn't want to use a potion or a spell to sleep. Despite all the apparent benefits of these methods—or so people claimed—she always felt more tired after using either one. It was all-natural sleep or nothing for her.

Her phone rang, and she pulled it hastily out of her pocket.

DAD.

She drew a deep breath. Sometimes, he could have the best timing. She'd sent him a text earlier asking him to call when he had time but to ask Davion to ensure their conversation was private. Davion was an infomancer who worked for the Brownstone Agency in LA. James didn't care for the laid-back man much, but since he rarely personally worked bounties anymore, he didn't have to deal with him so his opinion didn't raise issues.

"Hey, Dad," she answered. "Thanks for calling. You didn't have to do it today, but I appreciate that you did."

"I didn't wake you up, did I?"

"No, no. I was already up. This call gives me something to do."

"Glad I can help then," he rumbled. "This line's secure and all that shit, but what do you need to talk about that needs that level of security? Is this more dark wizard shit?"

"I wish it were that simple." She sighed and wiggled into a more comfortable position. "And no. I doubt any dark wizards will bother me or Izzie for a long time."

"What is it then?"

"I ran into a strange group recently called the Tapestry,"

Alison explained. "I eliminated a major force of them with the help of my main team, but that was far from the end of the organization."

"Fuck that. It's like with bounties. When the groups have some special name like the Council or Tapestry, they're ten times as annoying." James grunted.

"That's the thing, Dad. I don't even know what the deal is with these guys. They are strange and have some interesting magical consumables they use that enhance their bodies. Between what I sensed and what Hana smelled, there are too many questions we don't have good answers to. They could be humans with magic or Oricerans with unusual magic, but they also could be aliens with magic or aliens using magic-like tech. They wanted Omni, and that led to some…violent disagreement."

"They wanted the shape-changing pet?" James sounded surprised. "Why?"

She took a deep breath. "I suppose there's no other way to say this—he kind of turned into a seven-foot-tall killing machine when Hana's life was in danger. The Tapestry kept saying he was dangerous, but the only ones he killed were the guys attacking Hana."

"Huh. Shit. He could teach Thomas a thing or two," James replied. "And, what, you think he's alien and these Tapestry guys are, too? Maybe intergalactic bounty hunters?"

"I don't know, Dad. Maybe. I'm not sure. Everything we know from the Nine Systems Alliance says that aliens don't have magic, right? That we only have magic on Earth and Oriceran."

"Yeah, that's why those fuckers are so obsessed with me

—Earth and Oriceran." Her father chuckled. "They couldn't even do shit to stop a few portals when they all thought they could blow LA up with me in it. All their fancy-ass warships that can boil our seas, and you gather a few dozen magicals together and they're totally vulnerable. I guess I can see why they're pissing themselves about it."

Alison leaned her chair back a little more. "So that's it. I find it hard to believe that this powerful alien government would never see magic and then suddenly, other aliens show up, and they use it so casually it's like it's nothing. These Tapestry guys had heard of the Alliance, but they didn't seem to know what it was. I don't know if they heard of it on Earth or Oriceran or if they're from somewhere else entirely."

"Huh," James mumbled. "Maybe they aren't aliens, then."

She sighed. "I honestly don't know. The thing is, I can't even begin to get to the bottom of this without the help of my people, and I can't get them to help me properly if they don't know the truth, but it's not my truth to tell. I have involved the PDA, but they have so much bureaucratic red tape, and I'm not prepared to tell anyone in the government who doesn't already know about you. These Tapestry guys are bad news. They act like they care but they almost killed Hana, and they also made it clear they don't care about killing innocent people."

"Fuck it. If you trust someone to have your back in a fight, you can trust them with my secret. I don't really give that much of a shit if people know I'm an alien." James snorted. "It's the government that's so obsessed with keeping that shit secret. Johnston's told me all kinds of reasons why, but I still don't get it. Dumb government control crap."

"Thanks, Dad," Alison replied. "I'm not sure what the deal is with Tapestry, but it'll help my people to at least know where to look and where not to look." She laughed quietly. "You know, I feel like an idiot."

"Why?" James asked.

"Because I somehow thought, with the Seventh Order defeated, that everything would be simpler. We'd do more normal-scope jobs. Yeah, I've had some weird one-offs, but I thought there wouldn't be anything hanging over me like that again for a while." She frowned. "Now, I have the Drow crap and Tapestry. I'm at war with an organization I don't even understand because my employee refused to turn over her pet who can change shape into a super-assassin."

"You make it sound like that's a bad thing," he rumbled, a hint of humor in his voice.

"You don't think it is?"

James chuckled. "Alison, I destroyed an entire international criminal organization because they killed my dog. They might have survived if they laid off me more, but my pet started the whole thing. Besides, if these Tapestry fuckers are willing to kill without any kind of restraint, they don't deserve to have either a shape-changing pet or a killing machine."

Alison laughed. "The James Brownstone simple wisdom."

"Just saying. If you need help, I'm more than willing to come. I don't give a shit if they're aliens, magicals, or something else. They fuck with my family, they pay. Simple as that."

"Don't worry. I've got this, Dad. We already destroyed the local Tapestry nest. I'm sure they'll lick their wounds for a while. I want you to relax. You went straight from the Seventh Order to that stuff in Denver, then Christmas." She cleared her throat. "Since everything went okay with Christmas and meeting his parents, certain other things may be moving along. I can't guarantee anything, but that's what it feels like."

"Don't make him do that epic shit. It's annoying."

She laughed. "No, I already told him when he's ready to simply do what feels right. I'm trying to follow your KISS philosophy in this case, but I'm not sure if the Drow or the Tapestry will allow it."

James growled his annoyance. "They better, or they'll regret it."

"Thanks, Dad. It's always good to know I have you backing me."

"Always, Alison. Always."

The story is far from over. Learn more about Omni and stay current with Alison and her team's adventures in KEEP YOUR ENEMIES CLOSER.

FREE BOOKS!

WARNING:
The Troll is now in charge.

And he's giving away free books
if you sign-up!

Join the only newsletter hosted by a Troll!

Get sneak peeks, exclusive giveaways, behind the scenes
content, and more.
PLUS you'll be notified of special **one day only fan
pricing** on new releases.

CLICK HERE

or visit: https://marthacarr.com/read-free-stories/

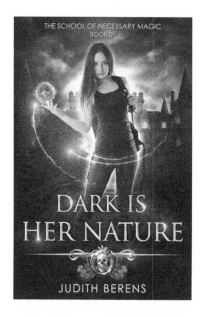

For Hire: Teachers for special school in Virginia countryside.

Must be able to handle teenagers with special abilities.

Cannot be afraid to discipline werewolves, wizards, elves and other assorted hormonal teens.

Apply at the School of Necessary Magic.

AVAILABLE AT AMAZON RETAILERS

AVAILABLE ON AMAZON AND IN KINDLE UNLIMITED!

I used to think that being a team player meant taking a back seat. Let someone else lead, unless the project was my idea – and then control everything. One route meant I had checked out and wasn't contributing as much as I could have and the other was stressful for everyone, including me – and I wasn't letting them contribute their spark of genius.

But fortunately, I wore myself out about a dozen years ago and went in search of a different way. Lots of sweat lodges, vision quests, spiritual self-help books, and talk, talk, talk. I was getting better-ish, but my anxiety was still pretty close to my hairline. Truth is, I was feeling better temporarily when doing these things, but I wasn't actually getting better. It was all temporary.

Oops, wait... Life had a different idea. Two years into my quest I was abruptly diagnosed with terminal cancer. The surgeon who I had just met five minutes earlier sat me down and said matter of factly, "You have a one percent chance of living longer than a year." I had no symptoms –

and frankly that's more often the case – but the end was near.

What really happened is I was getting the chance to turn my entire life around.

The effects were almost immediate. Instead of raising my anxiety, everything calmed down for me. I was about to check out and it was more important to me to clean up anything that needed it and leave on good terms. I mean, if I'm about to meet God, I'd like the meeting to go well.

I also got the chance to listen to other people's conversations about bills or lack of boyfriends, or bad bosses and I felt no connection to it. Instead I marveled that this was what ate up their time. I looked at what had consumed me for years in a new light and realized none of the bad things I imagined ever came to pass. It was wasted effort.

Two other really big gifts came out of it all as well. The first one was I stopped caring what other people thought. It stopped being my filter or my motivation. I really had no time left to babysit someone else's feelings and how they felt became their responsibility. You want to feel badly? Okay, I honor it, but I'm not tending to it. And I became more interested in people who were looking for a solution. Bad things might still happen, but they were dealing with it. They needed an ally and not a babysitter. I was on board.

The other thing was I got to assess where I was in life and whether or not I liked it. Were there regrets? Keep in mind, this was at the tail end of the Great Recession and I didn't have much. I had also been published traditionally to some great praise, been a national columnist but no real financial success. If I found a five-dollar bill in my purse it felt like I'd won something. And yet, I loved where I was because I was being true to myself and I may not have gotten to everywhere I wanted to be, but at least I was on the road. No regrets. Imagine getting a glimpse like that.

Then, the phone call came, and the nurse was more shocked to tell me than I was to hear it. They couldn't explain it, but the new tests showed I had gone into spontaneous remission. No one knew why or how long it would last. They felt comfortable raising my odds to a thirty-five percent chance, and I felt like dancing. I had gained thirty-four points! Then when I stayed in remission for a while, they raised my odds to fifty-fifty. I thought, well, it's time to get back to life. Looks like I'm going to live.

Sure, I had just as much chance at that point of dying as I did at survival, but those seemed like pretty good odds after one percent. And that ability to look toward the solution, to get back to what I can be doing – has stuck with me. I celebrated by jumping out of a plane and sailing through the sky.

Here's what I got out of all of it. I have no idea what the future is bringing – and I can choose to anticipate something good or dread something bad. I'm going with the good and if it's something I don't like instead, I'll deal with it – in the company of other like-minded people – and we'll find solutions and let go of the rest. There's not enough time to do all the wonderful things I'd like to be doing to waste any on fretting over things that haven't happened, or stuff I don't have any control over. I'm going back to living.

Postscript: Since that first bout, I've had cancer six

more times and I'm still out here kicking ass, having a grand time, getting into things all the time. Why not? The Offspring refers to me as a one percenter and it's a good reminder. The odds may be with you – what do you want to be doing? And if they're not, I'll be gone and won't be worried about it then, either. More adventures to follow.

AUTHOR NOTES - MICHAEL ANDERLE
JUNE 25, 2019

THANK YOU for not only reading this story but these *Author Notes* **as well.**

(I think I've been good with always opening with "thank you." If not, I need to edit the other *Author Notes*!)

RANDOM (*sometimes*) THOUGHTS?

So, if you have been around enough of our books (those between Martha and me), I refer to these types of author notes where Martha explains something amazing in her life as Author Note Blocking.

Because, how the heck do I top that? I can't. I've been too blessed in my life (I've never had cancer, don't want it, and frankly never want it. So Martha has taken the hits for the team here.)

The idea behind an author note blocking is that her author notes are so compelling, I really can't top them.

So, I come up with something frivolous (usually). Like…

Best comments about donuts. Here are three I particularly like:

1) Donuts - an excuse to have cake for breakfast.

2) How about it isn't you cheating on your diet with donuts, but rather you are cheating on your donuts with a diet.

3) Nothing tastes as good as skinny feels... Except donuts. Donuts taste like skinny can go F*** itself.

Dammit, now I want donuts.

AROUND THE WORLD IN 80 DAYS

One of the interesting (at least to me) aspects of my life is the ability to work from anywhere and at any time. In the future, I hope to re-read my own *Author Notes* and remember my life as a diary entry.

La Puente, CA, USA

I'm sitting at the kitchen table typing up these notes, having been stung by a wasp (on the neck) earlier this morning?

Why? Because I sent a couple of streams of wasp spray into their nest (somewhere behind a hole that went into my attic.

I was about thirty feet away, thinking I was far enough...until that one headed in my direction.

I didn't think I still had that amount of pick up the feet and put them down quickly until that moment. I swear I don't remember the distance between where I was standing and the gate going out beside the garage. That damned wasp followed me all the way to the trash can. where I thought I had lost it.

Until I felt something on my neck.

The sting wasn't too bad. I think I got it before it gave

me the full whammy. My wife put on some hydrocortisone and I left to go to Home Depot.

Like the man I am.

(There's nothing like killing a nest of wasps and dueling nature to make you feel all testosterone-y and stuff. When I came back, there were still two or three buzzing around the nest area.

I left them alone and went inside.)

FAN PRICING

$0.99 Saturdays (new LMBPN stuff) and $0.99 Wednesday (both LMBPN books and friends of LMBPN books.) Get great stuff from us and others at tantalizing prices.

Go ahead. I bet you can't read just one.

Sign up here: http://lmbpn.com/email/.

HOW TO MARKET FOR BOOKS YOU LOVE

Review them so others have your thoughts, and tell friends and the dogs of your enemies (because who wants to talk to enemies?)... *Enough said ;-)*

Ad Aeternitatem,

Michael Anderle

JOIN THE ORICERAN UNIVERSE FAN GROUP ON FACEBOOK!